"No more games, Jenny," he said. "It's just you and me now."

"It's been just you and me all along."

He looked at her mouth, at those tempting red lips. "Maybe you're right."

"Do you want me, Kyle?"

Her words stirred the fire in his groin, but he held back. "I think you know the answer to that." He moved closer, drawn to her despite his determination to keep his distance. "But that's not the real question, is it?"

She tilted her head slightly, obviously considering his words. "No, I guess not."

"Can you do this, Jenny? Can *we* do this? Can we make love tonight, and when this is all over, go our separate ways again?"

He heard her sharp intake of breath.

Taking a step closer, he wished he could lie, but knowing—this time, at least—she needed to hear the truth. "We live in separate worlds, Jen. Nothing's going to change. You know that, don't you?"

"Yes."

"Tell me no, Jenny. For both our sakes."

"I don't know if I can."

WHAT ARE *LOVESWEPT* ROMANCES?

They are stories of true romance and touching emotion. We believe those two very important ingredients are constants in our highly sensual and very believable stories in the LOVE-SWEPT line. Our goal is to give you, the reader, stories of consistently high quality that may sometimes make you laugh, sometimes make you cry, but are always fresh and creative and contain many delightful surprises within their pages.

Most romance fans read an enormous number of books. Those they truly love, they keep. Others may be traded with friends and soon forgotten. We hope that each LOVESWEPT romance will be a treasure—a "keeper." We will always try to publish

LOVE STORIES YOU'LL NEVER FORGET
BY AUTHORS YOU'LL ALWAYS REMEMBER

The Editors

RUNNING
FOR
COVER

PAT
VAN WIE

BANTAM BOOKS
NEW YORK · TORONTO · LONDON · SYDNEY · AUCKLAND

RUNNING FOR COVER

A Bantam Book / September 1997

ISBN 0-553-44617-7

Published simultaneously in the United States and Canada

Bantam Books are published by Bantam Books, a division of Bantam Dou-
bleday Dell Publishing Group, Inc. Its trademark, consisting of the words
"Bantam Books" and the portrayal of a rooster, is Registered in U.S. Patent
and Trademark Office and in other countries. Marca Registrada. Bantam
Books, 1540 Broadway, New York, New York 10036.

PRINTED IN THE UNITED STATES OF AMERICA

OPM   10 9 8 7 6 5 4 3 2 1

New ventures often need a certain
amount of luck
and a lot of help to get off the ground.
This book is dedicated to the three
women who made
writing for Loveswept a possibility for
me:

Sandra Chastain, for getting things
started;

Meg Ruley, for believing;

&

Shauna Summers—you'll be missed.

Special thanks to Gin, Ann, Debi,
Donna, and Sandra again
for putting up with me and my dreams
week after week.

ONE

They'd found her.

Jennifer Brooks knew it the moment she stepped into the reception area outside the school office and saw the two men. For five years she'd lived in relative obscurity, alone and away from the harsh focus of her former life. She'd taken another name and found a sort of peace teaching in a private girls' boarding school on the outskirts of Atlanta.

Now that was over.

Both men wore dark suits and stark white shirts, with telltale bulges beneath their jackets. She'd spent too much of her life surrounded by similar men not to recognize them. They had their own unique way of occupying a room: apart, alert, and ready. She also realized they merely provided the muscle. Whoever had sent for her, taking her out of her classroom in the middle of a school day, waited inside.

Bracing herself, Jennifer nodded to the men and walked into the office. The headmistress, Margaret Abrahm, rose as she entered.

Jennifer hardly noticed.

Instead, she saw only the man, silhouetted by the bright sunlight streaming through the windows, his back to the door. She didn't need to see his face to recognize him, nor question how he'd found her. He'd been the one person who'd always known her location; she should have realized he'd be the one to come for her. And maybe some part of her had.

"Thank you for coming, Jennifer," Margaret said. "This gentleman is from the U.S. Marshals Service. He needs to speak with you."

Jennifer nodded to the other woman without glancing at her. There was a limited number of reasons why he'd show up here, and the two deputies in the outer office ruled out the only good possibility.

"Deputy Marshal Kyle Munroe, I believe." Somehow she managed to keep her voice cool and unconcerned.

He turned, as if on cue, and Jennifer's control slipped.

It was one thing to recognize him from across a room while he kept his back to her. And quite another to face him. Lord knew she'd imagined it, dreamt of it, often enough. She should have been prepared.

She wasn't.

Seeing him like this, after all these years, was

harder than she'd ever expected, and it nearly took her breath away.

"Hello, Jenny." His voice wrapped around her, as warm and seductive as a moonlight kiss. And just as familiar. "How have you been?"

Five years. It should have been enough time to have gotten past her automatic reaction to him, to the longing created by just the sound of his voice. It wasn't. But she'd be damned before she'd let him see it. "What are you doing here, Kyle?"

A flicker of response sparked in his eyes—those devastating blue-green eyes that had once stolen her heart. Then the spark vanished, and he said to Margaret, "Could I have a few minutes alone with Miss Brooks?"

She hesitated and glanced at Jennifer, who nodded. "It's okay, Margaret. Deputy Munroe and I are old . . . acquaintances."

A moment later they were alone.

Neither of them spoke, but the memories drifted between them like misty phantoms. So much had changed since they'd last spoken, since they'd last touched. Jennifer was no longer the innocent, idealistic young woman he'd once known. He and her father had made sure of that. But Kyle . . . Well, the differences in him were more visible.

The years had aged him, broadening him across the chest and shoulders and painting a hard edge to his features. He'd once been boy-next-door handsome, with dark hair, eyes the color of a summer sea, and a smile that never failed to turn heads. Jennifer doubted whether women so openly watched him now. Not that he wasn't still handsome, or that they wouldn't be drawn to him. It was just that no one would mistake this dark, dangerous stranger for an easy man.

Jennifer broke the silence. "Why are you here?" she repeated.

"Your father sent me."

She let out a short, humorless laugh and crossed her arms. "You'd think he would have found someone else." She and Kyle hadn't parted on the best of terms. Letting the sarcasm drip from her voice, she added, "Oh, I forgot, he *had* to send you. You're the only one who knew where to find me."

"Your father trusts me." Kyle kept his voice cool and his gaze level, as if unaffected by her sarcasm.

It spurred her on. "Actually, I'm surprised you forced yourself to leave his side."

"Neither of us had a choice. There was nothing more I could do for him."

She dug her nails into the palms of her hands, resisting the sudden fear lashing at her insides. "Is he . . . "

A flicker of compassion crossed Kyle's features, the first real emotion he'd displayed, and for a moment he seemed more like the man she'd once loved. "Your father's safe."

Jennifer closed her eyes briefly and let the relief wash through her. It had been the same five years since she'd seen her father, and for a moment she'd thought . . .

"Jenny?"

She opened her eyes and met his gaze head-on. "I'm not going back."

"That's not why I'm here." He paused, and then said, "But there is a problem."

She fought the flush of regret at his answer. After all, she'd known better than to think Kyle had come for *her*.

"What do you know about Philip Casale?" he asked, shattering any lingering question about whether he'd come in a professional capacity.

"You mean, Vittorio Casale's son?"

"Yeah."

"I don't know much." She tried to remember what she'd heard. Vittorio Casale was possibly the most notorious and untouchable crime lord of the decade. Anyone who paid attention to world events knew the authorities had been after him for years. But there hadn't been much about his son, Philip; not until recently anyway. "All I know about Philip," she said, "is that he was convicted of counterfeiting a few months ago."

Kyle slipped his hands into his pockets, and for a moment didn't say anything, as if uncertain where to start. "Philip's a whiz kid," he said, finally. "A genius, by all accounts. He used high-end computer graphics and printers to produce the currency. Then he sold it to foreign governments.

"But that's only the beginning of what he's been

doing for his father. Though so far, no one has been able to prove anything beyond the counterfeiting." Kyle paused again, and then added, "Vittorio has plans for his son, and for using his genius to move the family business into the twenty-first century. And those plans don't include a jail sentence."

"Okay . . ." Jennifer prodded.

"Philip's case is up for appeal."

Jennifer caught her breath. "And Father . . ."

". . . is trying the case."

"I see." Jennifer released her breath and walked over to the leather couch and sat down. She didn't think she could take much more of this conversation standing up.

Three key witnesses and one juror had died mysteriously during the course of the original Casale trial. Still they'd convicted him. Now her father, Circuit Court of Appeals Judge Crawford Brooks, known as the "Crusader," would hear Philip's appeal.

"Why haven't I heard anything about this?" she asked.

"The appeal was made public yesterday, but we managed to keep your father's name out of it. We thought we could keep it quiet for a few days at least. Unfortunately, Vittorio has his own sources."

Jennifer hadn't heard the news yesterday. She'd gotten home late from an outing with a group of students. But she knew that as soon as the appeal had been announced, Vittorio Casale would have wanted to know who would try his son. And men like Casale usually got what they wanted.

"Vittorio wants his son acquitted," Kyle said. "He wants it very much." Jennifer met Kyle's gaze, praying she was wrong about what he was about to say. She wasn't. "Vittorio has made that clear to your father."

Jennifer steeled herself and resisted the urge to wrap her arms around her middle. "Father has received threats before."

"It's serious this time," he said.

She smiled wryly, wondering if Kyle realized how foolish his words sounded. As if all those other times, other threats, had meant nothing.

"Casale is ruthless," Kyle said. "And he has the power to carry out his threats."

"Will Father back down?"

"You know better."

Yes, she knew better. Her father never backed down.

He had his causes, his campaigns to single-handedly rid the country of crime. In the circles where he moved, many—especially Kyle—considered him a hero. But what good was a dead hero? Jennifer had wanted a father, and when she met Kyle, a husband. A normal life. But neither of the men she loved had been willing to give her what she wanted, while she . . . she hadn't been willing to live from day to day not knowing which one might be their last.

But that was ancient history.

"Okay, so why are you here?" she said once again.

"Your father has been taken into protective custody," he said. "And he sent me to you."

"Why?"

"He thinks Casale will try to use you as leverage."

"But no one knows where I am, and no one here knows *who* I am." She threw a glance at the closed door. "At least they didn't, until you showed up here today."

"Casale's men are good," he said uneasily. "Too good."

A sliver of fear slipped down her spine. She ignored it. "So, what are you saying? You're here to act as my bodyguard?" She pushed off the couch and stood. "No thank you, I've been down that road before."

"It's worse than that," he said. "I'm here to take you into custody as well."

"No." She'd responded automatically, yet she knew the minute the word escaped that it meant nothing. If Kyle Munroe and her father wanted her in protective custody, she'd have no choice.

"Staying here will endanger everyone around you," he said. "Staff, faculty, even the students."

Jennifer met and held his gaze. He wasn't fighting fair, and they both knew it. He could force this on her, but he wanted her agreement. Her cooperation. And he knew she wouldn't take a chance on endangering anyone else. Especially the students.

"Jenny—"

"Don't call me that," she snapped, then instantly regretted the outburst. He'd always generated emotions in her that no one else could touch. She didn't want anyone to ever have that kind of power over her again. Especially Kyle. "It's Jennifer."

He frowned. "I know you're angry, Jen . . . Jennifer, but—"

"Yes, I'm angry." She suddenly realized she'd never stopped being angry. At her father. At Kyle. They'd both chosen their work over her, and that work had once again put them all in danger. "You brought them to me. You told them where they could find me."

"It was necessary."

"For whom?"

"For your safety." He moved closer. Too close. It was always a danger with Kyle, letting him get close, listening to his voice, gazing into those eyes of his, eyes that begged for understanding while he once again tore her life apart. "Casale's men are the best I've ever seen."

"You always told me *you* were the best. That when you made someone disappear, they stayed that way."

Again the barest flicker of emotion lit his eyes, but it vanished almost before she recognized it. "Your father and I decided—"

"That's the problem, isn't it?" Anger gave her the strength to put distance between them again.

"It's always been Father and you deciding what was best for poor little Jenny." She glared at him from a safe distance. "Well I've got news for you, Deputy Munroe. I'm all grown up, and I make my own decisions now. I've been making them for five years. I don't want or need you or my father making them for me."

Kyle sighed and ran a hand through his hair. She noticed for the first time the weight of years that had settled on his face. He looked tired. "We don't have much time, Jenny. We need to get you away from the school. Are you going to cooperate?"

"I have no alternative, do I? Now that you've come here with your private army, Casale will be able to find me too." She waited a moment, though again, there was nothing he could say to change things. "I have to come with you or risk not only my own life, but those of the people around me."

For a moment he didn't say anything. She searched his face for some sign of regret, some flicker of guilt for the position he'd put her in. After all, he, of all people, knew how much she hated this, how much she wanted—no, needed—a normal life.

"I won't apologize, Jenny," he said, and there was a finality, a flatness to his voice she'd heard before. *I believe in what your father is doing,* he'd once said to her. *And I won't leave him.*

She knew from his tone that she'd lost, as she had five years ago, and the fight drained out of her. Nothing had changed between them.

"Okay," she said. "I need to get a couple of

things from my classroom and stop by my house. If I have to go into exile, I want my own clothes and personal things."

Kyle's first impulse was to refuse her. So far he'd kept his temper in check, but his patience was wearing thin. Jenny had pushed and argued, letting her resentment flare between them, while he couldn't afford the luxury. Still, he understood her anger. Stopping at her house wasn't a good idea, but it probably wouldn't hurt either.

"Okay," he said. "But you'll have to be quick about it."

"I know the drill." She turned and headed for the door.

Taking a deep breath, he followed her into the outer office. "DeMitri, Cross," he said to the men who'd accompanied him from Washington. "Escort Miss Brooks to her classroom to pick up her things. I'll go over procedure with Mrs. Abrahm and meet you at the main entrance."

Talking to the headmistress was an excuse. What he really needed was a few minutes alone; time to adjust to seeing Jenny again, time to reconcile himself to the hostility in her eyes.

Five years had changed her, left her even more beautiful than he remembered. And more distant. There had been no welcome in her eyes when she'd seen him, nothing to indicate she might still have feelings for him. There had been only anger at him and fear for her father . . .

Kyle stopped the thought before he could carry it further.

He refused to be jealous of her feelings for her father, or bothered because she'd found a new life for herself away from both of them. Hell, he'd helped create that life for her.

Now he'd destroyed it.

But he didn't have time to sort out the past—if it were even possible—or be concerned that he'd turned her life upside down again. His concern and focus needed to remain on the present, on keeping Judge Crawford Brooks's daughter alive. Something he was going to need all his skill and training to accomplish.

After a few brief instructions and reassurances to the headmistress, he headed for the school's main entrance. Two other deputies, on loan from the Atlanta office, had been waiting there. They'd provided a safe house north of the city and the extra manpower needed to guard it.

Jenny arrived a few minutes later with DeMitri and Cross in tow. Kyle mentally shook his head at the way she led the two men, rather than the other way around. It hadn't taken her long to fall back into the role of daughter to one of Washington's most powerful men. If they weren't careful, DeMitri and Cross would be stumbling over each other in no time, just to run her errands.

"Are you ready, Ms. Brooks?" he asked, distancing himself from her with a simple address.

"As ready as I'm going to be, Deputy." She met

his gaze, her eyes as cool and remote as if they'd never met. And that's exactly the way he wanted it, he reminded himself.

Indicating the Atlanta deputies, he said, "One of these officers will drive your car. You'll be riding with DeMitri, Cross, and me."

"I'm perfectly capable of driving myself," she said.

"No doubt. But you'll come with us anyway." He nodded to the other men; the matter was settled.

Taking her elbow, Kyle slipped his other hand inside his jacket. DeMitri and Cross took up positions on either side of them, while the two Atlanta deputies moved in front and behind.

Kyle scanned the area once more, and said, "Let's go."

He felt her initial resistance to his hold, but she did as he instructed. Again, she'd succumbed to old habits. It wasn't the first time Kyle had protected her from her father's enemies. He only hoped they'd both make it through this one alive.

They drove in caravan formation. The deputy in Jenny's car led the way, followed by Kyle, DeMitri, and Cross in the car with Jenny, and the second Atlanta deputy bringing up the rear. It wasn't a long drive, but to Kyle it seemed interminable. He tried to keep his eyes off Jenny, sitting as far from him as possible in the backseat of the government sedan.

He may as well have tried to stop breathing.

Again and again he found himself staring at her,

tracing the fine bones of her face with his eyes, noticing the new, shorter length of her hair and marveling, as he had in the past, that there could be so many different shades of gold. And there were her hands; long-fingered and graceful, clasped in her lap, the only outward sign of the tension running through her. He would have liked to reach over and take them in his, to pull them to his face and feel their softness once more against his skin. And if not that, he wanted to hold them and give her at least that much comfort.

She, on the other hand, seemed immune to him, keeping her face turned toward the window. Except once. She turned suddenly, and the deep brown of her eyes gentled and warmed for the space of a heartbeat. A brown-eyed blonde. He used to tease her that their whiskey color betrayed her true self. Abruptly, her eyes darkened, hardened, chilling him to the core. He knew then he'd been wrong about the color of her eyes. Brown could be every bit as hard and cold as blue.

A few minutes later they turned into a quiet suburban development. The deputy driving Jenny's car pulled into the driveway, while Cross and the third driver parked on the street.

Kyle knew this neighborhood. And this house. Five years ago when Jenny had wanted out, he'd found it for her. Still, it looked different than he remembered. It stood alone at the end of a cul-de-sac, a two-story brick surrounded by trees and backing up to woods. Large for one woman, the place was small compared to the mansion Jenny had grown up in. When he'd first seen this house, it had been new and empty looking even from the outside. In five years she'd changed it, put her stamp on it. Flowers bloomed everywhere: on the porch, in window boxes, lining the driveway.

He remembered she'd always had a green thumb, but somehow he couldn't picture the elegant Jennifer Brooks down on her knees, digging in the dirt.

"Looks like you've found a great gardener," he said, needing suddenly to touch some piece of her life. A life he couldn't be a part of.

"I don't have a gardener," she said, and reached for the car door.

Grabbing her hand, he stopped her. "Wait."

He climbed out of the car, followed by DeMitri on the front passenger side. They both made a quick visual survey of the area. Everything seemed quiet. Yet, something didn't feel right. Kyle glanced at DeMitri, who also seemed uneasy. "What do you think?"

DeMitri shook his head. "It looks okay." Though he didn't sound convinced.

Kyle circled cautiously around to Jenny's door, while checking on the other deputies getting out of their cars. Each one nodded in turn; they were ready for whatever instructions Kyle issued.

With his hand inside his jacket and resting on the butt of his gun, he once again looked at DeMitri.

"Let's get this over with," the other man said.

Kyle hesitated a moment longer, shaking off his uneasy feeling. His concern for Jenny was getting in the way of his better judgment. "Okay, let's go." Glancing around once more, he opened her door.

Jenny climbed out, and the world exploded around them.

TWO

Kyle threw Jenny to the ground, shielding her from the blast that showered them with charred debris, hissing and filling the air with the smell of smoke and destruction. He tightened his hold on her, keeping her head tucked down, away from the sight of her home engulfed in flames.

He held her there a moment, maybe two, long enough to know they were out of range of the explosion. Then without standing, he shifted away from her to open the car door.

"Get in and stay down."

For once she followed his instructions without argument, climbing into the car and lying down on the seat. He closed the door behind her and turned to check on the others. They had a man down; the deputy who'd driven Jenny's car and parked it next to her house. His partner, who'd driven the third car, had already worked his way up the driveway and pulled him away from the flames.

"Damn," Kyle swore. He should have listened to his instincts and gotten out of there the moment he sensed something was wrong. Either that or he should have refused to bring Jenny here at all.

"No way you could have known."

Kyle glanced at DeMitri, crouched, gun ready, a few feet away near the front of the car. He was right. They should have had plenty of time to get in and out before Casale's men found Jenny's house. Unfortunately, knowing that didn't make being wrong any easier.

Motioning toward the men nearer the house, Kyle said, "See what the situation is up there."

DeMitri nodded and headed up the hill.

Kyle stood and looked back through the car window to their driver. "Cross?"

He was already on the radio and held up a hand to indicate he was okay.

Kyle turned then to scan the area.

Except for the low roar of flames, everything remained quiet. Too quiet. And it made him uneasy. A few neighbors had come out after the initial explosion and stood warily in groups, talking among themselves, their hushed whispers adding to the feeling of unnatural stillness.

He glanced from the woods to the houses on either side of Jenny's; neither were close enough to be in danger from the fire. That also meant that whoever had set the bomb had probably gotten in and out without being seen. Either that, or he was still hiding back in those woods, watching his handiwork, waiting for Kyle and his men to come after him.

Kyle was tempted.

He could leave DeMitri here with Jenny and take the other two deputies into the woods. Whether they caught Casale's man or not, it would feel good to do something, to take some action against Casale instead of running and hiding. It would also be the perfect opportunity for Casale's men to grab her.

Frustrated, he ran his hand through his hair. As much as he wanted to catch this guy, Kyle's job was to protect Jenny. Because of that, he needed to get her out of here and to somewhere safe as quickly as possible.

Then he caught sight of her in the car. It had been too much to expect her to stay down. She sat watching her house burn, her face void of expression, as if the fire meant nothing to her.

He knew better.

The moment he'd seen the flowers, he'd understood what this place meant to her. It represented the life she'd always wanted, the control over her own destiny that had never been hers while living in her father's shadow. It was her future. Now that future had been jerked away from her. And again, he was responsible.

"He'll make it," DeMitri said from behind him.

Kyle turned, thankful for the distraction. "How bad is it?"

"A few cuts and scratches. Nothing serious. They said to go ahead. They'll handle the local authorities."

"Cross?" Kyle called.

"Help's on the way," came the answer, just as the sounds of distant sirens reached them.

"Let's go, then." Kyle opened the door. "We need to get Miss Brooks out of here."

As soon as Kyle and DeMitri were in the car, Cross took off. Fifteen minutes later they were safely away, heading north on Interstate 85. Jenny hadn't spoken a word.

"Are you okay?" Kyle asked.

When she didn't respond, he could no longer fight the need to touch her. Reaching over, he slipped his fingers through hers and enclosed her cold, stiff hand in both of his. He almost expected her to pull away, but she didn't.

"Jenny?"

"I'm okay," she answered, closing her eyes briefly before looking at him. It was almost his undoing. He saw her fear and her effort to control it, and the urge to take her in his arms swelled inside him.

"I'm okay," she repeated, as if reading his thoughts. And he wondered which one of them she was trying to convince.

"We've been through this before," he said,

tightening his hold on her hand. "We'll get through it again."

She bit her lip and nodded, but he read the doubt in her wide eyes and could guess her thoughts. There had been threats before, against her and her father, but the danger had always been one step removed. Even when she'd been forced to submit to a twenty-four-hour bodyguard, or taken temporarily to a safe house, it had never really touched her. She'd never been so directly endangered. It had never been this real.

"How did they find my house?"

Kyle wished he had an answer for her. "I don't know," he admitted reluctantly. "If Philip weren't in jail, I would say that he'd probably hacked into our files. As it is, he has no access to a computer. And no one, not even DeMitri and Cross, knew where you were today until I brought them to the school."

"And if Casale's men followed you?"

"That doesn't explain how they found the house, or had time to set a bomb."

She turned back to the window, and silence settled between them again. Then, with her eyes still on the passing scenery, she said, "It wasn't a mistake, was it?"

"What do you mean?"

"The bomb didn't go off prematurely." She still didn't look at him. "They weren't trying to kill me."

"No. It wasn't a mistake. You're no good to them dead."

She flinched. "Not yet, anyway."

He again tightened his hold on her hand, willing her to look at him. "It won't come to that, Jen. I won't let it."

Jennifer felt the pull of Kyle's voice and turned.

The intensity in his eyes surprised her, and for a moment she wondered if he still loved her. She quickly dismissed the idea. Kyle had made his choice five years ago; he'd chosen her father and his crusades over her. Since then, Kyle had never given her reason to suspect he'd regretted his decision. He'd deposited her in her new life and never once contacted her. There was no reason to think he'd changed his mind now.

She gazed out the window and forced herself to face facts. Protecting her was Kyle's job. He would do his best to keep her alive, but for Deputy Marshal Kyle Munroe it was nothing personal. Forgetting that would reopen old wounds, and she wasn't sure she could survive hurting like that again.

Resting her head against the seat, she closed her eyes. The movement of the car lulled her, and she let herself drift, her thoughts skittering about like unruly children.

Her house was gone.

Funny how she'd grown to love it when at first it had felt so cold and empty. It had taken time, but she'd made a home for herself, brought life to the cold brick structure. She'd made friends and populated her home with their laughter and confidences. Her students had often come over, bringing their hopes, their disappointments, their life. Now it was gone.

And Kyle had returned.

She felt his touch, his big hands cradling hers, offering her comfort. It occurred to her that she should pull away. Yet, she couldn't. Not when Kyle made her feel safe, and right now, she needed that more than anything.

Jennifer waited until full dark, in the cabin where Kyle and his men had brought her, and then she had to get out. She needed fresh air and some time alone to think.

Kyle had disappeared hours earlier, shortly after they'd arrived, so it was the deputy called DeMitri who tried to dissuade her. But the way she figured it, Casale's men either knew where she was or they didn't. Spending a few minutes outside on a balcony twenty feet above the ground, with no access except the door leading back inside, wasn't much of a risk. They weren't going to shoot her. They wanted her alive.

So despite DeMitri's objection she escaped.

Outside, the chilly night air surprised her. Earlier, the weather had been perfect, neither cold nor hot, but the comfortable temperature she'd come to associate with spring in Atlanta. She'd forgotten how quickly the warmth vanished once the sun set, particularly here in the mountains.

She considered getting a sweater but immediately dismissed the idea. She couldn't go back inside just yet. The walls had started closing in on her, and she wasn't sure she'd be able to bully her way past DeMitri a second time. So she ignored the temperature and walked over to lean against the railing.

It was beautiful here. And it should have soothed her.

The two-story cabin sat at the top of a gentle hill. Dark woods spread out in every direction and down to a lake, where the reflection of a quarter moon shimmered on its surface. No one had bothered to tell her their exact location, but she could guess. It was an isolated spot, about two hours north of Atlanta, on one of the many man-made lakes dotting the North Georgia Mountains.

In the past five years Jennifer had come to know and appreciate these mountains for their ancient beauty and tranquillity. Except now, that tranquillity was an illusion. Out among those silent trees, unseen men watched and waited, supposedly protecting her from her father's enemies. Somehow, she didn't think she'd ever find peace in these mountains again.

The door opened and closed behind her, and she barely suppressed a groan. She'd been hoping they would leave her alone for a while. Though she guessed that was too much to ask. She knew how protective custody worked. Until all this was settled with Philip Casale and his father, someone would be at her side night and day.

With that thought, a jacket was draped over her shoulders. Recognizing Kyle's touch, she stiffened.

"Here . . ." he said, his hands lingering a moment too long, ". . . it's getting chilly."

She pulled the jacket close and stepped away from him, away from the tempting warmth of him. "Thanks," she said, without looking at him. He'd been gone for hours, and she didn't want him to see her relief that he'd finally returned.

Settling against the railing, he said, "You shouldn't be out here."

"That's what Deputy DeMitri said."

"He's just trying to do his job. Like all of us."

She glanced sideways at him, but just as quickly turned away. In the dark he looked too much like the young man she'd once loved, and she needed no more reminders of their past.

"Where have you been?" she asked, keeping her voice casual.

He shifted next to her, leaning forward to rest his forearms on the wooden railing. "I had some things to take care of."

"Really?" She tried to keep the sarcasm out of her voice but failed. How typical of Kyle to answer her without giving away any information. If she pressed him, she knew he'd claim it was for her own good. He was only trying to protect her.

She should let it go. After all, why should she care where he'd been or what he'd been doing? He was nothing to her anymore, and she'd been perfectly safe there without him. DeMitri and Cross had hardly let her out of their sight. And of course, there were the men in the woods.

"You've been gone for hours," she blurted out, despite her determination not to. *And I was afraid you wouldn't come back.*

"I'm sorry." His voice crept past her defenses. As warm and deep as a summer night, it had the power to drag her back to another time—a time when she'd been far too vulnerable, far too easily distracted. "I didn't mean to frighten you."

"You didn't," she lied, but it came out in a breathy whisper she knew wouldn't fool him.

"Ah, Jenny . . ." He touched her cheek, his fingers like brands of fire against her skin.

The shock brought her to her senses, and she again stepped back out of his reach. "Jennifer," she corrected, chastising herself for even a momentary lapse while dealing with Kyle. She wasn't the same naive young woman she'd once been, and she wasn't going to let him evade her questions by distracting her.

"Are we safe here?" she demanded.

He remained motionless for a few seconds, before turning back to lean once more against the railing. "For now."

"For now?" She swung around to fully face him.

He'd changed from the standard issue dark suit, white shirt, and tie into a pair of well-worn jeans and plaid flannel shirt. He looked different, she realized. More like a good ol' boy than a federal marshal. She pushed the observation aside. "What does 'for now' mean? A day? A week?"

He glanced at her, but this time he was the one who looked away. "For as long as we need."

He was lying. She could hear it in his voice, see it in the stiffness of his back and shoulders. "I can handle the truth, Kyle."

For several heartbeats he kept his eyes on the lake and then turned to look at her. "Can you?"

It wasn't what she'd expected him to say, and an edge of fear crept into her voice. "Yes."

He glanced away again, past her into the darkness, his expression unreadable in the shadowy light of the quarter moon. "The Atlanta office assures me you're safe here." His gaze locked back on hers, and she knew the truth.

He didn't believe it.

It hit her hard. She'd known he was holding something back, but she hadn't suspected this. She'd thought they'd be safe here for a few days at least. Not that one place or the other made much difference while you were in hiding. It was just that leaving here meant things had gone from bad to worse, that Kyle no longer trusted the system he'd devoted his life to.

For a moment, she wished he'd continued lying to her. He could have assured her they were perfectly safe, that there was nothing to worry about. She wouldn't have believed him—not really. But she might have been able to sleep.

She turned away again, and this time let the silence float between them, tense and uneasy. Neither of them seemed willing to break it. But after a few minutes, she realized she couldn't take the quiet; it allowed the memories to fill the void.

"I've been thinking about buying a place like this," she said abruptly. "For the weekends."

She heard Kyle shift next to her, but didn't give him time to comment. "Melanie," she continued, "one of the other teachers at school, and her husband Joe have a cabin on Lake Lanier. It's not quite as fancy as this one, but it's nice. I've gone up there with them a few times."

"I'm glad you've made friends here, Jen."

She paused, wondering why she was telling him this. Then decided it was simpler than talking about crime lords or safe houses or moving on, far easier than talking about their past.

"They have a boat," she said, referring to her friends with the cabin. "Sometimes we water-ski. Mostly, I just walk in the woods."

"It doesn't seem like your kind of place."

She glanced at him briefly. "No? Well, maybe that was part of the problem. Part of why we never would have made it."

"Jenny—"

She held up her hand to cut him off. "Really, Kyle, I didn't mean to start an argument. I was just thinking aloud."

He seemed about to say something else and evidently thought better of it. After a few more moments of silence, he said, "So, you're planning on buying a place of your own. A cabin in the mountains."

"I was thinking about it." *Before everything changed. Before you came back into my life and destroyed it once again.* "Of course, I'll probably have to put it off now . . ."

"Jenny, I'm sorry about your house."

She smiled tightly and forced back a sudden wave of sadness. "Me too." Then, because she needed to return to a safer topic, she said, "Anyway, I thought a place in the mountains would be a great place to bring the girls."

"The girls?"

"My students."

"So you enjoy teaching?"

The question surprised her. "You know it's what I've always wanted to do. And yes, I love it."

For a few minutes, neither of them said anything, and she realized just how little they knew about each other. They'd been madly, passionately in love, but they'd never really known each other. Strange that she'd never realized it until this moment. All the hours she'd mourned losing him; the years she'd wasted waiting for him to come for her. And now, for the first time she realized maybe it had been a good thing that he hadn't. If they'd married, what would have happened to their feelings for each other?

"You never told me what made you decide to become a teacher," he said.

She looked at him sharply. "You never asked."

He had the grace to look embarrassed. "I always thought . . ." He shrugged and let his voice trail off.

"You thought teaching was just a whim. Something to idle away the time until I married and became a rich man's wife."

"No, I never—"

"Don't lie to me, Kyle."

He looked away, and she knew she'd hit it right on the mark.

"You thought it was a game to me," she said. "After all, good wives are well educated. So I went after a master's degree in education. So what?"

"I—"

Again, she didn't let him finish. "And what did you think you were to me, Kyle?"

He didn't answer. But then, he didn't have to. Jenny saw it on his face. He'd thought he was a rich girl's whim as well. A passing fancy. Someone she'd eventually get tired of.

"Well, I guess it just proves how wrong you were. About a lot of things." She turned and started to head inside, the night air no longer seeming as fresh.

"There'll be other teaching jobs, Jen," Kyle said, stopping her. "When this is all over, I'll set you up somewhere else."

She swiveled back around, and something inside her caught at the sight of him. And she lost all will to fight him.

"Yes," she said tiredly. "I'm sure you will. But for how long next time?"

Jennifer woke abruptly.

Turning her head to see the clock on the nightstand, she realized she'd been asleep for over three hours. She hadn't expected to sleep at all. The day had been too full of surprises. Too full of fear. She'd figured she would lie there and relive the events of the last twelve hours. Evidently she'd been wrong, because the last thing she remembered was lying down fully clothed.

And now she was awake.

For a moment she lay still and listened. She heard nothing; not even the night sounds of insects, or the movement of her guards in the outer room.

Yet, something wasn't right.

Something had jarred her from a deep, exhausted sleep.

Without giving fear time to take hold, she lowered her feet to the floor and sat up. Slipping on her shoes, she went to the window. She couldn't see a thing. The moon had set, and the darkness seemed almost too complete, too all encompassing.

Backing away from the window, she moved across the room and rested her ear against the door. Still, she didn't hear anything.

Cautiously, she turned the knob and opened the door.

A chair had been positioned outside in the hallway, where one of the deputies was going to sit all night.

It was empty.

Fear threatened to send her back into the room. She could lock the door, and she'd be safe until morning. Then she remembered Kyle telling her once that allowing fear to rule your instincts would only get you killed.

She stepped out of the room and scanned the hall.

Nothing.

Then from the darkness, a hard arm snaked out, grabbing her around her waist, just as a large masculine hand clamped down on her scream.

THREE

Jennifer threw herself against the iron hold, panic replacing thought. The arm around her waist tightened instantly, violently, forcing the air from her lungs.

"Quiet." It was a low hiss of a command, punctuated by a metallic snap and the feel of sharp steel pressed against her side. "I don't have to kill you to make you hurt real bad."

Jennifer went deathly still.

"That's it," whispered the voice. "Now, I'm gonna take my hand away from your mouth. But you ain't gonna make a sound. Right?"

She nodded, thoughts racing through her head, frantic and half formed as she struggled to grab on to them. Useless. She couldn't think.

The hand at her mouth loosened, then slid down to band her upper arm. She should scream. Ram her elbow into the gut behind her. Run. But it was like waking from a nightmare, desperate to scream with frozen vocal cords.

She couldn't move. She could barely breathe.

The arm at her waist slackened as well, sliding around until the flat of the blade became a dull pressure against her chest. Then the knife shifted again as the body behind her stepped back a fraction, holding her with the firm grip on her arm and the steady prick of steel at her side.

"Now we're gonna move real quiet down to that bathroom. And out the window. Got it?"

Again, she nodded.

Kyle? Where was he? And the deputy who'd been sitting at her door when she'd gone to sleep?

She started forward. One step. Two. And then she tripped, nearly falling. The hand on her arm jerked her back, but not before she saw the deputy sprawled at her feet, a pool of blood soaking the carpet.

Kyle kept to the shadows, inching closer to where the intruder held Jenny: one hand covering her mouth, the other wrapped around her waist . . .

Then he saw the knife. And froze.

Only one of Casale's men favored a knife. Billy the Blade. A trite, juvenile name for a deadly professional. Casale used Billy for silent work. He was good at it. And he enjoyed it.

Kyle faded farther back against the wall and

pulled his gun. It would have been an easy shot in the light, and without Jenny's shadow blending so tightly with Billy's. As it was, Kyle couldn't risk it—though it about killed him, with Jenny's fear calling to him and Billy's hands all over her.

With patience he didn't feel, Kyle watched as Billy moved his hand from her mouth, taunting her with the knife just below her breast while pushing her forward down the hall.

Then Jenny tripped, and Kyle saw his chance.

As Billy pulled her upright, Kyle sprang on him from behind, going for the hand with the knife, knocking it clear, half aware of Jenny stumbling backward as Billy whirled off balance to connect with Kyle's fist. Billy went down, started to bound back, and stopped—Kyle's 9 mm Beretta in his face.

"Come on, Billy," Kyle jeered. "Give me an excuse to blow your head off."

Billy sank back against the floor, hands spread. Obviously he wasn't ready to die.

"Jenny?" Kyle couldn't risk taking his eyes off Billy to look at her. "Are you hurt?"

It took a moment for her to answer. "No. I'm . . . okay." Her voice was shaky, but at least she could speak.

"DeMitri," Kyle called. "Get up here."

DeMitri showed up at the top of the stairs, gun in hand. Quickly sizing up the situation, he holstered his automatic and moved to Kyle's side. Grabbing Billy's hands and yanking them above his head, he cuffed them together around the railing. "How the hell did this scumbag get in?"

"Can't tell you," Kyle answered, though it worried him, almost as much as knowing he didn't have time to figure it out. Moving to the deputy on the floor, he pressed his fingers against the pulse point on the man's neck. "He's weak but alive."

"I'll do what I can for him," DeMitri said. Then, still speaking to Kyle, he nodded in Jenny's direction. "You better get going."

Kyle turned to Jenny, who had scooted away from them and sat against the wall with her arms wrapped around her knees. He wanted to take Billy's own knife to him, but he knew it wouldn't change anything; not the fear and shock on Jenny's face, nor what Kyle had to do next.

Going to her, he pulled her off the floor and into his arms. "It's okay," he whispered against her ear. It was all he could give her, all the comfort he had time to offer. "Jenny"—he stepped away from her—"we need to get you out of here."

"Why?" She seemed dazed. "What's going on?"

He wished he could tell her it was all over, that there was nothing more to be afraid of. But right now he needed her alert and cooperative. That meant she needed to know the truth.

"We lost contact with the deputies outside"—he threw a quick glance at Billy—"but not before we learned that Casale's men were in the woods."

The color drained from her face. "But—"

"Jenny, we're out of time." He couldn't let her go into shock. They needed to move. "Let's go." He took her hand. "Now." Without giving her time to protest, he led her toward the stairs, keeping to the shadows near the wall and away from the railing that overlooked the central room below.

He tried not to think of how small her hand felt in his, or how it trembled. He needed to curb his feelings. He'd almost lost it while watching Billy manhandle her. If he let himself get distracted by the woman, by his automatic response to her, they could both end up dead.

When they got to the top of the stairs, he stopped and motioned for her to stay put. He wasn't taking any more chances. Crouching low, he edged toward the railing. Cross was still below; a dark shadow near the front windows. Evidently sensing Kyle's presence, Cross looked up, nodded and raised a hand.

It was still clear. For now.

Back at Jenny's side, Kyle reclaimed her hand. "We need to hurry. There's no telling how long DeMitri and Cross can hold them off."

"But how?" The desperation in her voice tore at him. "If Casale's men are in the woods—"

"Hush." He pressed a finger to her lips, gently silencing her. "I'm not going to let them get you."

Her dark eyes searched his, looking for the truth in his words perhaps.

"You're going to have to trust me," he said, and moved his hand to cradle her face and stroke the soft skin of her cheek. "Can you do that, Jen? Can you trust me?"

It seemed an eternity—an eternity without air—before she nodded. It wasn't much, but it was enough. For now.

"That's my girl. Come on."

Still holding her hand, he started down the steps, moving quicker now, but again keeping close to the wall. On the first floor, he headed for the kitchen and the breakfast nook off to the side. Releasing her hand, he moved the table and flipped back the rug revealing a trapdoor beneath.

"It's a tunnel," he explained. "It leads out into the woods, about a quarter of a mile away from the house. It's our only hope of getting past Casale's men."

He lifted the trapdoor. The smell of damp earth rose up to greet him, and he involuntarily shivered.

"A tunnel, Kyle? Are you sure?"

Not many people knew about his dread of small, dark spaces, but Jenny knew. Though he'd always refused to talk about it or explain the source of his fear. It was a weakness; not something a man relished discussing—especially with the woman he'd loved. But she knew enough to understand what going down into that dark hole could do to him.

At the moment, however, he had no choice.

"It's fine," he assured her. Switching on the flashlight, he shone it down on rough wooden steps leading into the darkness. Handing the light to Jenny, he said, "I'll go first."

Bracing himself, he descended the stairs, and the first tendrils of discomfort reached for him. He pushed them aside. When he got to the bottom he held up his hand to her. "Okay, come on down."

She hesitated, glancing back at the living room where Cross crouched beside the windows. "What about the others? DeMitri and Cross? We can't just leave them."

"Casale's men aren't stupid. They're not going to kill federal marshals unless they're forced to. Once you're gone, DeMitri and Cross will be in a lot less danger. But we need to get moving. We're running out of time."

She hesitated a moment longer before descending the steps. Once she was down, Kyle handed her the flashlight and climbed back up to pull the trap-door closed.

The darkness settled around him, and he fought the rush of panic that came with it. He concentrated on his breathing. Slow and easy. He could do this. He *must* do this. Gradually, the terror receded to sharp-edged fear. And he could control fear.

He waited a few more minutes, until he heard the thump of the rug dropping back into place and the scratch of the table and chairs against the floor. Then he made his way back down the stairs and retrieved the flashlight from Jenny.

"Ready?" he asked.

Taking a step toward him, she lay a hand flat on his chest. "Kyle?"

He knew what she was asking. Could he do this?

Hell, he'd learned long ago that a gun at his back wasn't a good enough reason to crawl into a hole. But Jenny was. And right now, every minute counted if he was going to get her out of there alive.

"Stay close," he said in answer. "And be careful."

He started down the tunnel, ignoring the clammy feel of his hands, the closeness of the damp walls, and the threatening panic at the edge of his consciousness.

He moved quickly, with Jenny behind him, keeping the flashlight pointed at the ground in front of them. It felt like they walked for hours, like he'd never again see the open sky or feel a fresh breeze on his face. Then the tunnel ended abruptly, with a dirt wall and a ladder leading to another trapdoor above them.

This one hopefully led to safety.

Kyle shone the light on his watch. It had been a little over thirty minutes since he'd first lost contact with the deputies outside—though again, it felt like a lifetime. Now he and Jenny should be a quarter of a mile away from the house, but that didn't mean they were safe. He had no idea who waited for them beyond that door.

If Casale's men knew about the cabin, and had somehow managed to get inside, they could also know about the tunnel. But Kyle was betting they would have put someone down here if they'd known about it. They would have covered all the bases.

Jenny was too important to them; too important to their plans.

Turning, he slipped the Beretta from his shoulder holster and held it out to her. "Remember how to use this?"

Jennifer shifted her gaze to the gun. Years ago Kyle had taught her to shoot, but she'd never been comfortable with a weapon in her hand.

Taking a step back, she shook her head. "No."

"Sure you do." He followed her. "Take it, Jen."

She lifted her eyes to his, but could barely make out his features in the dark. Though she could imagine the grim set of his mouth and the determination in his eyes. "I don't want it."

"But you might *need* it."

No! she wanted to scream. She wouldn't need it. Kyle was here watching over her, and nothing was going to happen to him. But she knew he couldn't promise her that.

Reluctantly, she took the pistol.

Reaching behind him, Kyle pulled another gun from the waistband beneath his jacket. "Okay," he said. "I'm going up first and see if it's clear. I want you to stay back. If anything goes wrong—"

"Nothing's going to go wrong."

"If anything goes wrong, get back to DeMitri. He's a good man. And Jenny"—he nodded toward the weapon in her hand—"don't be afraid to use that."

"Kyle . . ."

"Hey." He touched her cheek again, another

warm caress that scared her as much as it reassured her. "It's going to be okay." With that he leaned over and kissed her; a light, devastating kiss that frightened her more than all her father's enemies combined. Then, just as quickly, he released her.

Stunned, Jennifer backed up. "What was that for?"

"For luck."

He turned and scrambled up the ladder. Near the top, he stopped and threw her a quick glance, and Jennifer realized just how much this trek underground was costing him. Maybe as much as the kiss had cost her. Then he shut off the flashlight and plunged them into complete darkness.

Jennifer held her breath.

The door creaked, and black became dusky gray as the natural darkness of night fell into the tunnel. She could just make out Kyle's silhouette—a dark shadow against the night sky—climbing up and out, weapon in hand. Then he vanished.

Her hand tightened on the gun he'd given her, and it took all her willpower to stay put. Everything was quiet. Still, she could imagine the worst; Casale's men waiting in ambush for Kyle outside the tunnel. A man with a knife . . .

No. She shook that thought.

Kyle had told her to go back if anything went wrong, but she wouldn't. She couldn't leave him there, to face alone whatever waited outside this tunnel. Nor could she return to that house, where a man who'd held a knife to her lay handcuffed to a wooden railing. She'd rather head up the ladder and see for herself if Kyle was okay.

Suddenly, he reappeared in the opening. "Come on up, Jen. It's clear."

With a sigh of relief, she tucked the gun into the waistband of her jeans like she'd seen Kyle do and headed for the ladder. She started up, taking his hand to make the transition from the top rung to solid ground. Then he lowered the door, and she helped him conceal it with branches and dead leaves.

Once they were done, she pulled the weapon from her waistband and held it out to him. "Here."

"Keep it for now. In case we get separated."

She didn't want to think of that possibility but kept the gun anyway, tucking it back in her waistband.

"Okay," she said, noticing him glancing around as if deciding which direction to take. "Where to from here?"

"Are you up for a hike?"

"Do I have a choice?"

He grinned. "This way." He took off in a direction she guessed would take them farther from the house, but downhill toward the lake. It wasn't the way she would have chosen.

"Wait," she said, catching up to him. "The road is uphill."

He nodded but kept walking. "And as soon as Casale's men realize we're gone, that will be the first place they'll look."

It made sense, and she did her best to keep up with him.

Neither of them spoke as they worked their way through the woods. At any other time, Jennifer would have thought the night unbelievably dark and still. But compared to the tunnel, it seemed almost full day and frantic with the noise of night creatures.

Suddenly, Kyle grabbed her arm and pulled her down behind some bushes. Too frightened to speak, she just looked at him. He raised the barrel of his gun to his lips, warning her to be quiet. It was an unnecessary gesture. Except for the pounding of her heart, she couldn't have made a sound if her life depended on it.

It seemed like they crouched there forever, hearing and seeing nothing. Still, fear kept its hold on her. Again, she looked over at Kyle, tense and ready, the pale glimmer of his gun, a deadly reminder of the danger they faced. She glanced down at her own hand, clutched around the weapon he'd given her, and couldn't remember when she'd pulled it from the waistband of her jeans.

That's when she heard the rustle of leaves off to their right. Then an electronic squawk, and she realized a man stood less than ten feet from their hiding spot. Dressed all in black, he'd blended in so well with the trees that she hadn't seen him until the call of his walkie-talkie had broken the silence.

Now he spoke into the handset, too low for her to hear his words—though she could have guessed at the gist of them. He was one of Casale's men, watching the woods in case she tried to escape. Finally, he refastened the instrument onto his belt and faded back into the woods.

Still, for several minutes, Kyle didn't move.

Then he nudged her and motioned in the direction they'd been moving before ducking out of sight. Without a word this time, she followed.

They walked faster now, downhill and away from the cabin.

Jennifer couldn't help but think about the deputies they'd left back in the cabin: DeMitri and Cross. Casale's man hadn't been looking for her and Kyle, he'd been watching. He didn't know they'd escaped. Which meant the men they'd left behind were still in danger. The guilt of it tore at her, though she knew there was nothing she could do.

Finally they came to the water's edge, and Kyle stopped.

"Now what?" she whispered, conscious of how easily sound carried over water.

Kyle seemed distracted, examining the bushes, obviously looking for something. "We're easy prey in the woods." He, too, kept his voice low. "But they can't track us over water."

Jennifer glanced toward the lake and shivered. She couldn't imagine getting into that dark, cold water.

"Don't worry, Jen." She could hear the amusement in his voice and wondered if he'd read her thoughts. "We're not going swimming tonight." He moved off without further explanation, keeping close to the shoreline.

Again, Jennifer was forced to catch up to him. "Then what are we going to do?"

"I hid a boat out here this afternoon."

That explained what he'd been doing when he disappeared, she thought. At least part of the time. She didn't even want to guess what else he'd been up to, but she had a feeling she was going to find out.

In a couple of minutes he stopped again and started pulling branches aside. When she realized he'd found the boat, she started helping him uncover it. When they finished, he slid the small flat-bottomed Whaler into the water.

"Okay," he said. "Climb in and curl up on the bottom. I'm going to cover you with a tarp."

"Is that necessary?" The idea of not being able to see where she was going frightened her.

Kyle sighed. "Yes, it's necessary. Casale's men are looking for two people, a man and a woman. We may not fool them for long, but at this point, every minute counts."

Reluctantly, she climbed into the boat and winced inwardly as she lay down on the cold metal bottom. Kyle handed her one of the flotation pillows for under her head and covered her with the tarp. She never would have admitted it, but the covering felt good after the chilly woods.

Then she felt him push off from the shore.

She couldn't guess how much time passed while Kyle maneuvered the boat and she lay hidden. But her discomfort faded quickly as the sounds of the stroking oars and the soft whoosh of water passing beneath the hull, lulled her. It reminded her of the boathouse on her father's summer estate, and the long hours she and Kyle had spent there, curled up in each other's arms, while water softly lapped against the pilings beneath the floor. Back then, she'd believed he would love her forever.

She'd been wrong.

She must have lost track of time, dozed perhaps, because the next thing she knew the boat eased to a stop and bumped gently against something solid.

A moment later, Kyle pulled off the tarp. "Are you okay?"

"Fine." Jennifer sat up, blinked, and instantly started shivering.

"Here." Kyle removed his jacket and handed it to her.

Nodding her thanks, she glanced around. They were in a small marina, tied off among dozens of other boats of various sizes.

"The worst is over." Kyle nodded toward a stone building at the top of the hill. "There's a Jeep waiting for us up in the inn's parking lot."

The simple ingenuity of his plan amazed her. An unidentifiable boat left among a dozen other equally anonymous boats. And a Jeep, ready and waiting, parked among others. She began to understand why Kyle was so good at his job.

He helped her onto the dock, and they made their way up the hill. As he'd promised, a Jeep waited for them. Soon, Kyle was negotiating the winding roads that snaked through the mountains, heading for the highway.

She waited until the dark terror she'd felt in the cabin had faded in the presence of open sky and asphalt. Then, turning in the seat to look at him, she said, "So, what do we do now?"

Kyle glanced at her, meeting her gaze for a moment before turning his attention back to the road. She could almost see him calculating how much of the truth to tell her.

"Now," he said. "We're on our own."

FOUR

Dawn hovered somewhere just beyond the rim of the Eastern Smokey Mountains when Kyle decided to stop. He picked a roadside motel on the outskirts of Chattanooga; a place where no one would notice one more set of tired travelers.

Leaving the car close to the front door, he let Jenny sleep while he registered and made a call from the pay phone in the parking lot. Then he drove around back, parked and turned to her.

He hated waking her.

He used to love watching her sleep. He would lie awake for hours, tracing her delicate features with invisible fingers until she finally awoke. Then he'd pull her into his arms, and they'd make love. Too many times during the last five years he'd wondered if he'd imagined it; that short, magical space of time when he'd called Jenny his. Now sitting in the dark, close enough to touch her, he knew that time had been real. And that it had passed.

Reaching across the seat, he touched her cheek. "Jen. Wake up."

She came awake with a start, her gaze locking on his, wide and wary. "What?"

"It's okay." He brushed a strand of hair from her mouth, longing to follow it with his lips.

"Kyle?" There were questions in her voice, in her eyes.

He couldn't stop himself, he leaned closer, his hands trembling as they caressed her face. "We're going to stop for a few hours. Get some rest."

For a moment she remained still, and he saw the memories in her eyes. Suddenly, she straightened, edging away from his hands. "Where are we?"

Disappointment flooded him, and Kyle shifted away feeling like a fool. He needed to remember just how poorly their relationship had ended. And that it had been his fault.

"Chattanooga," he answered, grabbing his duffel bag from behind the seat and climbing out of the Jeep. "I got us a room."

He headed up the stairs without waiting to see if she'd follow. She did, slowly, and he unlocked the door to the room and stepped aside to let her enter first.

Jenny took a few steps into the spartan room and halted. "There's only one bed."

Behind her, Kyle closed and locked the door before commenting. "We're registered as husband

and wife." He tossed the duffel bag on the bed. "Someone might notice if we'd asked for two beds."

"What about separate rooms?"

He met her gaze and arched an eyebrow. "What about them?"

They both knew he wouldn't allow her a separate room. Just as they both knew she'd objected automatically; a knee-jerk reaction to the memories he'd awakened back in the Jeep—memories of a different time, a different city, and a different motel room with only one bed. They'd shared *that* bed— though they hadn't gotten much sleep.

His body tightened at the thought, and he decided she had the right idea. Separate beds. Separate rooms. Hell, separate states would be safer.

"I'll take the floor," he said, and moved away from her, putting distance between them and their past. Crossing to the bathroom, he checked to make sure there was no window. Then he switched on the light and pulled the door partially closed, just as Jenny headed for the nightstand and reached for the lamp.

"Don't!"

She snatched her hand away.

Annoyed with himself, Kyle ran a hand through his hair. "Sorry. I shouldn't have snapped. It's just we need to keep the rest of the lights off."

Nodding, she folded her arms protectively around her middle.

He hesitated, her reaction disturbing him. Jenny wasn't the type of woman to jump at any man's command, especially his. But then, he didn't usually bark orders like a drill sergeant. Nor had he ever known her to back away from a fight. If he was behaving like an overbearing ogre, he would have expected her to come right back at him.

Unusual as it seemed, he pushed the observation aside. They were both overtired and on edge. And there were more important things to worry about than Jenny's behavioral patterns.

Retracing his steps back to the windows alongside the door, he examined the locks. They wouldn't stop a determined twelve-year-old from getting into the room, but they'd have to do. For tonight anyway. After one quick glance at the deserted parking lot, he pulled the curtains tightly closed and turned back to Jenny, who hadn't moved.

"Are you okay?" he asked.

A thin ribbon of light from the bathroom cut across the room behind her, making her seem like a dark, immobile statue in the dimness. "Are we safe here?" she asked, instead of answering his question.

His automatic impulse was to protect her—even if it meant stretching the truth. "Yes," he said. "No one followed us."

"How long this time?"

The question took him aback. Though it shouldn't have. Less than twelve hours ago they'd stood on a balcony in North Georgia, and he'd told her they'd be safe for as long as they needed.

Four hours later, they'd been running for cover.

"We'll stay the night and head out tomorrow afternoon," he said. "Get some sleep. You'll feel better in the morning."

"I want a shower first."

He nodded his agreement and turned back toward the windows. "Make it quick." Then, almost as an afterthought, he added, "There are some clean clothes in the bag that should fit you."

After a moment, he heard her rummaging through the bag, then the bathroom door closed, plunging the room into darkness.

He breathed a sigh of relief.

Alone in the dark, without Jenny's presence to distract him, he could think more clearly. He could put aside questions of how to treat her, or memories of what they'd been to each other, and concentrate on the danger that faced them. He could plan how to keep them both alive.

Pulling back the curtains, he checked the parking lot once again. Everything was quiet.

He'd taken a risk coming to Chattanooga.

Logically, he should have stuck to the main highway and headed south to Atlanta or north into South Carolina. He could have traveled faster and had them safely tucked away in a motel room just like this one a lot quicker. Or they could be on a flight to some distant city. Of course, Casale's men would have been right behind them. And Kyle had no intention of providing such an easy target.

He'd figured they had one shot at losing Casale's men, and taking the logical route wasn't the answer. So he'd gambled and headed due west, taking narrow two-lane roads that meandered across the North Georgia Mountains. It had taken more time, and if their pursuers had guessed his strategy, there would have been no place to hide.

He'd taken a calculated risk that had paid off. So far.

No one had followed them, and it bought Kyle the time he needed. Time to rest, regroup and plan. He estimated they had twenty-four hours before anyone thought of Chattanooga. By that time, he and Jenny would be long gone.

Dropping the curtain, he pulled off his shirt and stretched out on the bed. They'd get a few hours sleep, and by noon tomorrow the call he'd made earlier should produce results. Then they'd be safe.

As long as they stayed on the move.

Suddenly he realized Jenny was still in the shower. Sitting up, he glanced at his watch. Twenty minutes. A little too long for comfort. Crossing the room, he knocked on the bathroom door. "Jenny? Are you all right?"

No answer.

He pushed open the door. "Jenny?"

When she still didn't respond, fear coiled in his gut. In two strides he crossed the room and pulled back the shower curtain. She stood under the onslaught of water, head bent, arms wrapped around her middle, shaking.

Fresh, raw guilt slammed through him.

Delayed shock. After dragging her from her

safe, normal world, he should have seen it coming. He should have helped her through it. Instead, he'd let his memories get in the way.

Cursing himself, he shut off the water, grabbed a towel and draped it around her shoulders. He lifted her from the tub; it was like handling a limp doll. "I'm sorry, Jenny. This is my fault."

"No," she said, a soft desperation in her voice. "You don't understand."

"It's been a hell of a day. You're frightened. But everything's okay now. We're safe here."

He used a second towel to rub her dry, attempting to warm her trembling limbs while ignoring the way his body hardened at the feel of her soft, feminine curves. Not thinking clearly had gotten them into this mess. If he'd been paying attention, it would never have gotten this far.

He wasn't going to make the same mistake again.

"I'm going to take care of you, Jenny. I promise. Leave everything to me."

She shook her head. "Not me. Those men. DeMitri and Cross. We left them there to—"

"No." He couldn't let her finish the thought, though he feared the same thing. As long as Casale's men thought Jenny was in that cabin, they would keep coming. And if two deputy marshals got in their way . . .

"No," Kyle said again, more to himself than her. Grabbing the T-shirt she'd hung on the doorknob, he pulled it over her head, covering the temptation of her body. "They're fine."

"You don't know that."

"They're good men. They know how to take care of themselves." He prayed it was true as he worked on her hair, drying it as best he could by hand.

She clutched his arm, stopping him, forcing him to look into her eyes. He saw her pain and guilt over having left those men behind in order to escape. "Are you sure?"

Dropping the towel, he lifted her into his arms. "Yes," he lied. "I'm sure."

He carried her into the outer room and gently set her down. Keeping one arm wrapped tightly around her waist, he pulled back the spread and helped her into bed. Then he crawled in beside her, pulling her close and covering them both with the blankets.

A moment later, her tears came.

Survivor's guilt. It was something he understood all too well. And there was nothing he could do but hold her.

"Shhh." He pressed his lips against the top of her head, letting them linger on the damp silk of her hair. "It's okay, Jen. I'm here. Sleep now."

Eventually, she did.

Jennifer drifted slowly toward the light with a sense of rightness she hadn't experienced in years.

She lay snug against a warm male body that seemed infinitely familiar and different all at the same time. Sighing, she pushed herself closer, loving the way his body responded to hers.

"You keep on rubbing against me like that . . . no telling what might happen."

The sleep-husky voice snapped her awake, and she nearly tripped over herself scrambling out of the bed.

Kyle laughed softly. "Well, at least things are back to normal."

He'd risen partway, resting on one arm with a sheet draped carelessly low around his waist. His broad chest, bare and incredibly sexy, unnerved her further. "What do you think you're doing?"

"Minding my own business." He yawned expansively. "Until that sweet bottom of yours started twitching."

A flush of embarrassment rushed through her. "Why are you in my . . . ?"

Everything returned in a rush. Kyle and his men showing up at the school yesterday. Her house exploding. The faceless man with a knife. The damp, dark tunnel. The man in the woods. Kyle and her escape.

Then, she'd fallen apart.

Shivering, she ran her hands over her upper arms. She didn't remember where they'd stopped— the outskirts of some town or city—though she wasn't sure Kyle had even told her. She vaguely recalled climbing into the shower before everything went blank. Then there had been only a dreamlike awareness of Kyle, holding her through the night, his deep voice whispering assurances in her ear.

"I'm fine now," she said to no one in particular.

Kyle lifted an eyebrow, and another flush of embarrassment washed over her. "Look, Kyle, I'm sorry about last night. I didn't mean . . . I was just . . ."

"Exhausted."

She couldn't let herself off the hook so easily. "Yes, but it's not like me to fall apart like that."

"You had every right."

"No." She shook her head. As always, Kyle was trying to protect her from the truth. "I should have been stronger."

"You hung in there while it mattered."

She started to deny it, then stopped. His expression echoed his words and the truth of both. She *had* gotten through the worst of yesterday. It was only after they'd reached relative safety that everything had closed in on her.

Still, she'd spent the last five years learning to take care of herself, proving to Kyle and her father that she didn't need their protection. And she couldn't quite forgive herself for needing Kyle so badly last night.

"I won't let you down again," she said.

"You didn't let me down before."

She smiled tightly, suddenly aware that she wore only a thigh-length T-shirt. She started to fold her arms but realized that would only make the situation worse. Instead she said, "I better get dressed."

"Good idea." He threw back the covers, and she held her breath, releasing it only after she realized he still wore his jeans. He'd left the top snap undone and was making no attempt to hide his body's reaction to her earlier position. "I'll see if I can find some coffee."

Grabbing the clean clothes she'd meant to put on last night, Jenny escaped behind the closed bathroom door, Kyle's soft laughter trailing behind her.

When Jennifer emerged from the bathroom fifteen minutes later, she once again felt in control.

Until she spotted Kyle.

Sprawled in the room's only chair, legs crossed and propped on the edge of the bed, he looked more like one of the criminals he hunted than a federal marshal.

He wore the same well-worn jeans he'd had on the night before, but that's where the similarities ended. He'd exchanged the plaid flannel for a black T-shirt that molded itself like a second skin to the muscles of his arms and chest. A leather vest and boots, both well past their better days, seemed a natural extension of this new persona he'd taken on. As did his slicked-back hair held in place with a bandanna, the dark stubble shadowing his jaw, and the sunglasses. Mirrored. It fit him and alerted her to a different side, a hidden aspect of danger in this man she thought she knew.

He even moved differently. Bolder. With an arrogance meant to intimidate, he removed his sunglasses and rose from the chair, bringing with him a brown bag from the floor.

She took an involuntary step back.

"These," he said, tossing the bag on the bed, "are for you."

She picked up the bag but didn't open it, still too stunned by his appearance to do or say anything more.

"They're clothes," he said. "Put them on."

She glanced down at her wrinkled khaki slacks and blouse. "Is something wrong with what I'm wearing?"

His gaze raked her from top to bottom, sending shivers down her spine. "They're not right."

Jennifer hesitated a moment longer before opening the bag, pulling out a pair of worn jeans, a white tank top, and boots.

"There's a jacket—"

"I can't wear these," she said, looking up at him when she realized he'd given her the feminine equivalent of his clothes. "They're . . . too small."

"They'll fit."

She dropped them back on the bed. "I don't *want* to wear these, Kyle."

"Do you want to stay alive?"

The question stopped her, but only for a moment. "I suppose the next thing you're going to want is for me to climb on the back of a motorcycle."

"No." Kyle tossed her a second, smaller brown bag. "Next, you're going to do something about your hair."

"What?" She reached up and touched her hair before opening the small bag and pulling out a box of dark hair dye. "Why—?"

"Then," Kyle interrupted, "you're going to climb on the back of a motorcycle. Because that's the way we're traveling from now on."

FIVE

For a moment, Jennifer was speechless.

Not because it surprised her that Kyle planned on exchanging their getaway Jeep for a motorcycle. After all they'd been through, nothing much would shock her. It was because he was still giving orders without explanation and expecting her to obey without question.

Then he turned toward the door saying, "We don't have a lot of time. While you're working on your hair, I'll get us something to eat."

His voice snapped her out of her inertia. She tossed the box of hair color on the bed next to the clothes and crossed her arms. "Forget it," she said stubbornly.

That stopped him cold, and he swung back around, impatience and anger clouding his features. "Forget it?"

She refused to let him intimidate her. "I'm not

coloring my hair, and I'm certainly not getting on any motorcycle. Not until I get a few explanations."

"Really?" He crossed his arms, mocking her perhaps. "And if I don't *explain* things to you, what are you going to do? Hole up in this room until Casale comes knocking?"

With an effort, she checked her temper. As usual Kyle had dismissed her questions. Only this time he wasn't going to get away with it. So far she'd gone along with him every step of the way, following his every command without question. But they were in no immediate danger, and she wanted some answers.

"If those are the only options you're offering me," she said, "I'll put a call in to the local U.S. Marshals Service. I'm sure someone else will pick me up."

"And you'd be in Casale's clutches within twenty-four hours."

Fear slipped down her spine, but she ignored it and held his gaze. "I guess I'll just have to take my chances."

Neither of them moved for what seemed an eternity, and Jennifer thought he'd call her bluff.

Finally, Kyle shook his head and swore. "You don't get it, do you?"

Jennifer held her breath, afraid to believe she'd won. "Why not try explaining it to me."

He stared at her a moment longer, then shifted his eyes to focus on some unknown point behind her. "Every move we made yesterday, Casale's goons were one step ahead of us. At your house. At the cabin. Both places *should* have been safe. At least for a while."

Jennifer nodded. None of this was news to her. "Go on."

"Until I started operating alone." He looked back at her. "Yesterday afternoon I set up the boat and Jeep without informing anyone in the department. And we got away. That tells me two things. First, Casale's men aren't as good as they want us to think. And second"—he paused, as if not wanting to voice his next thought—"someone is feeding them information."

"What about Philip, the computer whiz?" Jenny asked. "Couldn't he have hacked his way into the Justice Department computer and gotten information to his father?"

"Possibly with the right equipment." Kyle hesitated. "But he's been locked up for the past six months, without even access to a PC."

"Are you sure?"

"That's what my sources tell me."

"Maybe your sources are wrong."

Again he hesitated, and she could almost see the idea taking root in his mind. "I'll have someone check into it."

"Okay," she prodded, "so for now you think it's safer for us to operate outside of the department."

"As long as we're on our own, I can keep you safe. I'm good at this, Jenny." He took a step toward her. "But you're going to have to trust me."

She lifted her gaze to meet his. "You keep saying that, Kyle. But I'm not the only one who's having problems with trust. You need to trust me as well."

He looked uncomfortable, but before he could say anything else, she asked, "Why the clothes and the motorcycle?" Though she had a pretty good idea what he had in mind, she needed to change the subject. She didn't want to explore the issue of trust between them, any more than he did. Not now.

For a moment he didn't respond, then he acknowledged her shift back to a safer topic with a nod. "The best way to disappear is to become someone else. No one is going to look for Jennifer Brooks on the back of a Harley." He picked up the discarded clothes and handed them to her. "Especially if she looks like she belongs there."

Jennifer dropped her gaze to the clothes. It was safer than looking into the blue-green depths of Kyle's eyes. "And my hair?"

He reached out and lifted a strand from her shoulders, and his voice softened. "It's too noticeable."

The feel of his hand in her hair was almost more than she could take, and she had to fight the impulse to step back. She looked up, again feeling the pull of his stare.

"All right," she said, leaning over and picking up the box. "I've always wondered what it would be like to be a brunette. Looks like I'm about to find out."

He lifted his eyebrows in disbelief.

"Go get us something to eat." She pressed the clothes and hair dye close to her chest like a shield.

"Just like that?"

"I'm not suicidal, Kyle," she snapped, though she hadn't meant to. If only he weren't standing so close, with those searching eyes of his slipping past her defenses. "I just want you to start talking to me, tell me your plans. This is *my* life on the line here, and I want to be included in the decisions."

He seemed to consider her words for a moment and then nodded. "Okay."

Jennifer smiled, despite herself. "Go on. I'm starved."

With a smile, he turned and started toward the door.

"Kyle, wait," she said, stopping him once again. "What you said last night about DeMitri and Cross . . ."

"They're fine, Jen, really."

"No more lies, Kyle."

"Okay, you want the truth?" He tunneled his fingers through his hair before dropping both hands to the waistband of his jeans. "DeMitri and Cross knew the risks when they became federal marshals."

"Nothing personal. Is that it?"

"That's right. It's part of the job. And last night, well, they knew their chances of making it out of that cabin."

"You don't think they made it."

Kyle hesitated before saying, "Not unless Casale's men figured out we were gone before they raided the cabin in force. But if they'd figured that out . . ." He shrugged, not finishing his sentence.

But he didn't need to; Jennifer knew the rest. "If Casale knew we'd run, we wouldn't have gotten away."

He pressed his lips together and nodded. "I made arrangements with DeMitri. He's supposed to call me at a predesignated number tonight. We'll know then if they made it."

"And my father?" He'd been on her mind since she awoke this morning, but she'd been afraid to ask. "Can we contact him?"

"Your father's not in danger, but calling him will endanger us."

She studied his face, his eyes, trying to decide if he was lying to protect her once again.

"Hurting your father won't help Casale," Kyle explained. "The court would only appoint a different judge, and it would go even harder on Philip." He paused, and she knew for once he was telling her the whole truth. "It's you they want, Jenny. Not your father."

For several minutes after he left, Jennifer just stood there. His last words should have disturbed her, but strangely they comforted her instead. Her father was safe. And she had Kyle to watch over her.

She looked like sex.

Kyle dropped his feet to the floor and started to

stand, until he realized his legs might not support him at the moment.

Stepping out of the bathroom, with the only light in the room coming from behind her, she was every man's fantasy—all wrapped up in skin-tight denim and clingy knit. She'd made herself over into a loose woman—just as he'd planned—and he hated it. He didn't want any other man looking at her dressed like this. And they *would* look.

Her jeans left nothing to the imagination: not the wickedly long length of her slender legs, nor the provocative curve of her backside. While that top made a man's fingers itch to touch, to feel the weight of those full, rounded breasts in his hands. Kyle hardened at the thought and shifted in a vain attempt to ease the pressure.

He had an irrational urge to make her change into something more appropriate—something tailored and loose fitting like she usually wore. Either that, or throw her down on the bed and make love to her for the next week or two.

She took her time walking toward him, stopping just short of touching distance. "How do I look?"

She'd done the makeup too. He hadn't thought about that—though he should have. She'd painted her lips whore-red and worked some kind of feminine magic on her eyes, making them larger, darker, beckoning. And her hair, her sweet honey-colored hair that a little while ago had whispered of class and breeding, now hung loose, dark and sinful about her shoulders.

He rose, careful not to touch her. "You'll do."

Her gaze dropped to his crotch, and a knowing smile teased her lips. "I kind of like it myself."

Grabbing the leather jacket from the bed, he shoved it toward her. "Here. Put this on."

"Will I need it?"

No, I will. "It gets cold on the back of a bike."

"What about you? Aren't you going to get cold?"

He stepped away from her toward the door. "I'll be fine. Now, let's get out of here."

She laughed softly, a dark, sultry sound that sent a fresh wave of fire to his groin. "Sure. Let's go."

She followed him out of the room and waited as he locked the door behind them. Then she led the way down the stairs, her hips swaying in a way he'd never noticed before. In the parking lot, she stopped in front of the black Harley.

"This it?" she asked.

Kyle pulled out his keys and swung his leg over the seat. "This is it."

"You know, I've never been on a motorcycle."

"Lesson one." He settled into the seat and shifted the bike off its stand. "It's a bike. *Not* a motorcycle."

"Sorry." She crossed her arms, and he tried not to notice how the motion tightened that already too-tight top across her breasts. She hadn't put on the jacket yet. "So, where did you get it?"

He started to tell her not to worry about it, but as he opened his mouth he saw the warning in her eyes. She'd asked for the truth. Well hell, if she wanted truth, that's what she'd get.

"I made a call last night and had a friend deliver it along with the clothes," he said. "In exchange for the Jeep. Now, put on the jacket."

"Someone in the department?"

He let out a short laugh as he kick-started the Harley. "Does this look like government issue?"

She looked the bike over from front to rear, as if not knowing what to think of it. "It looks like—"

He revved the engine, cutting her off. "The bike's mine," he said over the low rumble. "A friend was keeping it for me. Now, are you coming or not?"

An hour later, Kyle decided that riding with Jenny clinging to his back was almost as bad an idea as having her put on those clothes. She'd taken to both surprisingly well—too well.

After some initial stiffness, she'd fallen into the rhythm of the bike—her body flowing easily with his as they took to the road. They threaded their way along the outskirts of Chattanooga, through miles of roadside construction and midday traffic before emerging northwest of the city. Then the highway stretched out, wide and empty in front of them. By then, Jenny rode like a pro, like she'd been sitting behind a man in leather, on the back of a Harley, all her life.

No problem on her part.

He was the one with the problem. It had nothing to do with her ability to go with the motion of the bike, and everything to do with the way her thighs pressed against his, and the feel of her soft breasts against his back.

The sign had once blinked *Samson's* in neon blue, but the *S*'s had ceased functioning years earlier, which hadn't made a heck of a lot of difference. Samson's clientele weren't the kind who needed a sign to find the place.

Pulling off the road onto the gravel lot, Kyle maneuvered the Harley into a narrow sliver of space between two choppers. He killed the engine, and the sound of Garth Brooks singing about having friends in low places replaced the bike's muffled rumble.

Letting down the kickstand, he shifted around to look at Jenny, amused by the sheer disbelief on her face. She might wear those clothes like they were made for her, but underneath, she was still a Washington society girl. And in every way that counted, Samson's was a dive.

A low, dilapidated wooden building, the bar was a biker's haven in bad need of fresh paint and a new roof. And from the looks of the vehicles parked outside—a few battered pickups and a rundown car or two, amid a dozen bikes of various makes and models—it could use a new clientele as well. At least, he figured that's how Jenny saw it.

"Hungry?" he asked.

"Not for food poisoning."

Kyle laughed lightly. At least she hadn't lost her sense of humor. "Hasn't killed me yet."

"You've actually eaten here?"

"On occasion." He swung off the bike and offered her a hand. "They have the best ribs east of the Mississippi."

"*Are* we east of the Mississippi?" She ignored his hand and managed to climb off on her own, but her legs gave way beneath her.

Kyle grinned and caught her around the waist. "Easy there. Might take a minute or two to get your land legs back. And yeah, we're still east of the Mississippi. Though not by much. We're north of Memphis a bit. Maybe twenty miles from the river."

Jennifer let him steady her. Actually, she didn't have much choice. After seven hours on the motorcycle, her back and legs ached from top to bottom. She doubted whether she'd ever walk normally again, and at the moment, they didn't even seem inclined to hold her up.

It had been worth it, though. It had been a wild, exhilarating ride, and she'd loved every minute of it. Of course, she'd never admit that to Kyle. Not in this lifetime, anyway.

"You okay?" he asked.

Though still sore, her legs felt steadier now, so she untangled his arm from around her waist and stepped away. "Yeah, thanks."

He smiled and nodded toward the building. "Let's go, then. There's a man inside I need to see."

"Wait." She grabbed his arm but instantly released it. The feel of hard muscle beneath cool skin only made her more unsure. She was out of her element here, and she *really* didn't want to go into that place. "What do I do?"

His gaze slid down the front of her, the heat of it stroking her as surely as if he'd used his hands. "Just remember how you're dressed. And act the part."

"That's easy for you to say. You look like you were born in those clothes."

"Believe me, sweetheart"—the soft purr of his voice added heat to the fire he'd started with his eyes—"so do you."

She pulled the leather jacket closed and shook off the sensation. "I don't think I—"

"You did just fine this morning."

Her cheeks heated at the memory of how she'd flaunted herself in front of him earlier. "That was . . ." *That was for you.* But she couldn't say that aloud. "That was different." Though she had to admit she liked the feeling—then and now—the power to make him want her. The way he once had. Of course, there was danger in that—like playing with a lit match.

"Look, Jen, people don't ask a lot of questions in a place like this." He draped an arm around her shoulders. "So, just stay close, and you'll do fine."

She glanced at his arm, remembering her thoughts about the danger of fanning old flames. "Is that necessary?"

"With you dressed like that . . ." Again, his eyes raked her from head to toe. "I want to be sure every man inside understands who you belong to." There was an intensity to his voice that surprised her, stirring another hot flame of awareness low in her stomach. "That way, no one's going to mess with you."

She would have liked to argue, but couldn't. Not with his eyes on her like that. Besides, it felt good—no, safer—with Kyle's arm around her. Though that was something else she'd never admit to.

"Okay." Her voice came out shakier than she'd have liked, but there was nothing to be done about it. Hopefully he'd interpreted it as nerves. "Let's go."

"Just relax." They started toward the door. "You'll be fine."

"Who could you possibly need to see here?" she asked, more to distract herself from the thought of actually entering this place, than to know the answer.

"The owner. He's the man who kept the Harley for me."

Jennifer mentally groaned as Kyle led her across the dark parking lot toward the entrance of the raunchy bar called Samson's. She wasn't sure whether Kyle's answer made her feel better or worse about going inside.

Until they pushed through the door.

SIX

The inside of Samson's struck Jennifer full force.

The smells hit her first—stale beer and tobacco. Then, as her eyes adjusted to the dim light, sights took shape: the crude wood floor covered with sawdust, the dozen or so mismatched tables and chairs, the long bar backed by rows of bottles in front of a grime-covered mirror. And the crowd, dressed mostly in frayed denim and well-worn leather, showing lots of tattoo-covered skin, all seeming to have a great time beer guzzling and foot stomping to the twang of country music.

It was enough to make any sensible woman turn on her heel and head on down the road. Unfortunately, Kyle had a strong grip on her shoulder, so Jennifer wasn't going anywhere. She tried to relax as he'd suggested, but didn't have much success.

"Hey, you! Munroe!"

Jennifer stiffened, and Kyle turned slowly

toward the bar and the biggest man she'd ever seen. He had to be six seven at least, with shoulders the width of two men and arms the size of another man's thighs. A full head of wild, strawlike hair hung to his shoulders, and a beard, as bushy and unkempt as the hair on his head, added to the image of massive strength.

Folding those oversized arms across his broad chest, he glared at Kyle. "You got a lot of nerve showing up here." His deep voice carried over the din, though no one else seemed to care or even notice.

"What about you?" Kyle answered, his voice equally loud, equally challenging. "Showing that ugly face of yours in public?"

Jennifer caught her breath.

The man *was* as ugly as he was big, and for a moment she thought he'd vault the bar and come after them. Then he let out a deep-throated roar of laughter and motioned toward the back of the room. "Delilah's at the corner table. Take her place and tell her to get herself back to work. Her break's over."

Kyle grinned and lifted a hand in mock salute.

Only then could Jennifer breathe normally, as she realized it had all been in jest. Still, it took her a minute to calm her fear. Men, she thought, as Kyle led her through the crowd. They were no better than overgrown boys: testing and teasing.

When they reached a round table tucked in one

of the back corners of the bar, Kyle stopped. "Hey there, gorgeous, I've got a message from the man."

"I heard him," said a tiny, hard-looking blonde sitting at the table. "No doubt everyone in the whole damn place heard him." Grinding out her cigarette in an overflowing ashtray, she stood and directed her raised voice toward the bar. "He forgets I own half the place. And you . . ." She turned back to Kyle and cuffed him on the cheek. "You think you can just waltz in here anytime you please and take over?"

"Come here"—Kyle grabbed her and lifted her off her feet—"and give me a proper welcome."

The woman smacked him on the back with her fists. "Put me down."

Laughing, Kyle set her back on the floor but kept one arm firmly tucked around her shoulders. "Good to see you too, Delilah."

Pulling away from him, she straightened her clothes and nodded toward Jennifer. "So, are you going to introduce us?"

"Jenny," he said, still grinning, "meet Delilah. Samson's better half."

Delilah snorted her disgust at his obvious flattery. "I always said you were full of it, Munroe." Then to Jennifer, she added, "But *you're* welcome. Even if Munroe, here, was the one who brought you."

"Thank you," Jenny said, too overwhelmed to think what else to say. "It's nice to meet you."

"Hah!" Delilah rolled her eyes, produced two

bar napkins from her pockets and slapped them on the table. "So sit, both of you, and tell me what you want."

Kyle laughed again. "A couple of drafts"—he nodded toward the chairs, and Jenny claimed one— "and two rib specials. Full slabs."

"You got it." She started to leave, then turned and gave them an almost-smile. Suddenly she didn't seem so hard anymore. " 'Bout time you brought yourself back in here, handsome."

Kyle's smile softened in response, and Delilah moved off to fill their order.

"Samson and Delilah?" Jennifer said, turning to Kyle. She felt like she was still on the motorcycle, spinning out of control. The bar, Samson's greeting, Delilah and Kyle—especially Kyle—none of it seemed real.

He laughed lightly. "The story is, she turned up here looking for a job, took one look at Samson and called herself Delilah."

"And now she *owns* half the place." Jenny shrugged out of the heavy leather jacket and hung it on the back of her chair.

Kyle followed her movements with his eyes. "A woman can cause a man to do all kinds of stupid things."

The blatant suggestion in his voice stirred her, tempted her to bait him. Though she couldn't have said exactly why. Unless it had something to do with this place and how Kyle seemed to fit here, while she remained an outsider. Maybe she just needed to see something of the man she thought she'd known, force him to react in a way that was predictably Kyle.

"But not you, right?" she said. "Not the great Kyle Munroe, U.S. federal marshal. No woman ever sidetracked you. Made *you* do something stupid."

"Don't be so sure."

She let out a short, humorless laugh. "Come on, Kyle. Remember who you're talking to here. I'm the one you left for your career."

"*You* walked out on me."

"I walked out on a lifestyle." *And left my heart behind.* "I wanted you to come with me."

"You wanted me to give up everything I'd worked for."

"My point exactly." She forced a smile past the pain, wishing now she'd left the ghosts of their past alone. "You never would have given up half your place for a woman."

"Put the jacket back on."

Jennifer recognized the anger in his eyes and refused to back away from it. This was a different man from the one she'd known, but she was different too. Older. Wiser. And unwilling to be intimidated by a dark scowl and angry eyes.

"It's too warm," she said. "No one else is wearing a jacket. Besides"—crossing her arms on the table, she leaned forward, letting the neckline of her skimpy knit top dip lower—"I thought I was playing a part."

Kyle's gaze dropped to her breasts. "Be careful, *Jennifer*. You don't want to play your part too well."

"Why, Kyle . . ." She sat back and, with a flick of one hand, brushed her darkened hair away from her face. "I'm just doing what you told me."

Irritation flashed across his features, but there was desire as well. The combination sent a shiver of delight through her insides to settle low in her stomach. She leaned forward again, eager to push him just a little further.

Samson picked that moment to show up, carrying two mugs of beer and depositing them on the table. "Glad you could make it, Munroe," he said, grabbing a chair and sitting carefully, like an adult forced to use a seat designed for children.

It took Kyle a moment to shift his eyes from Jennifer to the other man. "Me too."

Samson's gaze flicked briefly to Jennifer but then settled on Kyle. "Did you find everything you needed?"

Kyle claimed one of the beers and took a long swallow before answering. "Everything was in the Harley's bags, just as I asked. And the Jeep?"

"Little tame for my taste, but Delilah's thrilled."

"Good. It's yours."

Samson nodded, as if he'd expected as much, and shifted his attention to Jennifer. Holding out a hand the size of a small ham, he said, "I'm Samson."

"Nice to meet you. I'm Jennif . . . Jenny." She

took his hand, and he cradled hers gently in both of his—like a man with a small child.

Grinning, he nodded in Kyle's direction without taking his eyes off her. "Don't suppose I could convince you to forget this lowlife and take up with a real man?"

Jennifer returned his smile and threw a glance at Kyle. "It's tempting. Unfortunately our . . . relationship . . . goes back a ways."

"Too bad." Though still holding her hand, he looked at Kyle. "I like this one. Even if she does have bad taste in men."

"This one?" Jennifer turned a questioning eye toward Kyle, wondering how many other women he'd brought to this place. Had they all been forced to dye their hair and wear clothes a size too small?

"You talk too much, Samson." Kyle's voice remained calm, but his eyes issued a warning. "And I think it's about time you took your hands off her."

Samson laughed but pulled back. "No harm meant."

Kyle nodded, his eyes never leaving Samson.

Again, this was another side of Kyle; one she'd seen hints of earlier in the day when she'd first seen him in his biker clothes. A very dangerous side. She'd always known about his job, the risks he faced on a daily basis and the training involved in becoming a U.S. marshal. Yet, she'd always seen him as calm, professional, efficient. Now, suddenly she realized that even a man of Samson's size would think twice about going up against Kyle Munroe.

"Look . . ." Jenny stood, needing a few minutes alone to sort things out and try and come to terms with all these different aspects of a man she once thought she'd known inside out. "I'm going to take a walk."

Kyle started to rise. "I'll go with you."

"Relax, Munroe," she said, emphasizing the use of his last name while pushing him back into his chair. "I can handle this myself. Besides, it might look a bit odd if you followed me into the ladies' room."

"Still, it's not—"

"The lady's safe," Samson said. "No one causes trouble in my place."

Jennifer believed him and smiled her thanks. Then, before Kyle could dredge up any further objections, she headed toward the rest rooms.

Kyle watched the sweet swing of Jenny's hips as she wove her way through the crowd. He should have ignored both her and Samson's objections and gone with her. He knew she was safe—at least from Casale's men. He'd never have brought her here otherwise. But he didn't like the way a dozen pairs of male eyes followed her across the room. Once again, she'd adapted well. Too well for his comfort.

"This one is personal."

Samson's voice brought Kyle's thoughts and gaze back to the table. "In my line of work, there's no such thing as personal."

Samson laughed shortly but stopped as Kyle leveled a warning stare in his direction. The big man feigned intimidation by raising his hands palm out in surrender. "Whatever you say, Munroe. It's just a job."

Kyle couldn't afford to care, to let his emotions get in the way. At least that's what he'd been telling himself for the past two days, since he walked into that school and took Jenny into protective custody.

Too bad he wasn't listening.

Taking another swallow of beer, he changed the subject. "Any messages?"

Samson's smile faded, and he shook his head. "Sorry."

Kyle took a deep breath, hope dying within him. He'd been carrying it around since he and Jenny had escaped from the safe house the night before, leaving DeMitri and Cross behind. DeMitri was one of the best deputies Kyle had ever worked with, and he was a friend. It looked like he hadn't made it.

"Okay, then," Kyle said, more to himself than Samson. "Time to move on. We need a place to stay for a few days. A week at the most."

"No problem." Samson reached into his pocket, pulled out a key, and slid it across the table. "You know the way to my cabin."

Kyle nodded. "Where will you be? In town at Delilah's?"

"She's likely to raise a fuss. You know how she likes her own space. But she'll get over it. Besides . . ." He grinned. "She owes me for the new Jeep."

Kyle laughed, feeling a flash of envy for the simplicity of Samson's life. He and Samson had each chosen their own road, and in some ways Kyle's had been the easier choice. He'd have to be content with that.

Just then Jenny emerged from the ladies' room and started back toward the table, only to be stopped by a tall biker near the bar. Kyle watched as she smiled at the man in a way that sent a surge of jealousy straight to his gut. He was out of his chair before he could think.

Samson's deep laugh followed Kyle across the room, but he ignored it. He stopped behind the biker, who was giving Jenny some song and dance about what a great guy he was. She seemed to be enjoying herself just a little too much.

Then her gaze met Kyle's, and the biker turned. "Hey, man, this one yours?" He nodded toward Jenny.

"That's right."

The man looked back at Jenny in appreciation. "Well, if I were you, I'd keep a closer watch on her. No telling when someone might try to steal her."

"If I were you"—Kyle edged closer to the other man—"I'd mind my own business."

The man took a step back, raising both hands palms out. "Chill. No cause to get uptight. I didn't mean nothing."

"Like hell you didn't." Kyle grabbed Jenny's arm and drew her past the biker. "Come on."

She only let him pull her a couple of steps before she yanked her arm from his grasp, fire in her eyes. "What the hell do you think you're doing?"

He could think of only one way to stop the flare of temper building in her eyes. Slipping an arm around her waist, he guided her into the crush of bodies on the makeshift dance floor.

"I think"—he took her wrists, drawing them to his shoulders—"it's time we dance."

Jenny's eyes sparked with defiance as she started to back away. He stopped her, his hands circling her waist and pulling her hips against his.

"Relax," he whispered, finding the silky skin beneath her shirt and edging her closer. "This is a game, and we're just playing our parts. Remember?"

He watched her resistance slip away as her eyes darkened, the sweet honey-brown changing to something challenging and infinitely more alluring.

"Oh, that's right. A game." She smiled slowly, enticingly, and Kyle instantly realized his mistake. Rising on her toes, she clasped her hands behind his neck and brushed her freshly reddened lips against his. "And two can play as well as one."

Kyle nearly groaned aloud, his body hardening as she rubbed her pelvis against the front of him. "Be careful," he growled against her lips, while his hands seemed to move of their own accord, finding the back pockets of her jeans and slipping inside to hold her against the ache in his groin.

"I'm always careful," she answered, and once again lifted her lips to his. This time in invitation.

He didn't disappoint her. Couldn't. He'd fantasized about her lips for years, wondering if they could possibly be as sweet as he remembered.

His mouth took hers, claimed hers in a rite of possession as old as Adam and Eve. And it was so much more than he remembered. Jenny answered in kind, taking as much as she gave, meeting his tongue with her own, while driving her hands into his hair.

Kyle's control crumbled away.

It had always been this way between them, fast and explosive. And Kyle knew it would be so easy to let himself go, to forget everything except the feel of her: the rounded curve of her backside beneath his hands, the fullness of her breasts pressed against his chest, the eagerness of her mouth, and the hard, aching need between his thighs.

Then the music changed.

A hard-driving beat replaced the seductive rhythm of the country ballad. Jenny didn't seem to notice, but he did, and it snapped him back to his senses. As he broke the kiss, anger drove past his desire, and he pulled his control around him like a well-worn jacket.

Shifting away from her enough to look at her, he said, "Are you done playing games yet?"

She lifted those dark, seductive eyes of hers to his, while her lips curved into a knowing smile. "What's wrong, Kyle? Suddenly you don't like the rules?"

"I don't think you understand what's at stake."

"Still trying to protect me?" Her voice mocked him, as she slipped out of his embrace. "From who this time? You? Or myself?" Without giving him time to answer, she turned and walked away, leaving him standing there alone.

For several moments he didn't move, while desire and anger fought their petty battle within him. He couldn't lie anymore. He wanted her. As much or more than the first time they'd met—nearly six years ago. They'd been in her father's chambers, and from that moment until the day he'd left her in Atlanta, she'd drawn him into her heart and her life.

Only now, the stakes were higher.

Jenny's life had been threatened, and it was his job to protect her. Neither of them could afford the distraction of desire. They were playing a dangerous game they couldn't win—no matter what happened with Casale. Because, the real danger was letting her into his heart again.

He needed to get them out of this bar, back to neutral ground. They'd slipped into their adopted roles too easily, and it had clouded his judgment. He, for one, needed to think clearly if either one of them was going to make it out of this alive. As for surviving each other, that was another problem entirely.

Ten minutes later, they were back on the bike heading toward Samson's cabin, a sack of uneaten food stored in the bike's saddlebags. The drive seemed to take forever, though it was only a little over five miles of rural highway, followed by another mile or so of dirt road leading deep into the woods.

Jenny had remained distant since he'd followed her off the dance floor, voicing no objection when he'd told her they were leaving. Now she sat behind him on the bike, as far away as physically possible, holding on with only her hands at his waist. It didn't matter. He'd have known she was there, felt the chemistry still arcing between them even if she hadn't touched him at all.

The road finally ended in a small clearing, occupied by a two-room cabin. Kyle drove to the back and shut off the engine, and the sudden silence of the surrounding woods descended like a heavy cloak.

He slipped off the bike but he didn't dare touch Jenny. Not as she climbed off herself, or as they made their way back to the front. He unlocked and opened the door, and she started to step inside but stopped, meeting his gaze in one long, searching look, before crossing the threshold. Then he followed her, closing and locking the door behind him, and waited.

He watched as she moved about the small room, looking, touching, exploring with her hands what she couldn't see in the dim light. He sensed her disquiet, her uncertainty. Her desire.

Finally, she stopped at the door to the bedroom. He couldn't make out her expression in the dark, but he pictured what she saw. Samson's massive bed, made for a man the size of a small mountain. Or a night of intense lovemaking.

As if hearing his thoughts, she turned and moved toward him, slowly, until she stood just within touching distance. Through the front windows, the moonlight fell across her face, rendering her features almost mystically beautiful.

"No more games, Jenny," he said. "It's just you and me now."

"It's been just you and me all along."

He looked at her mouth, at those tempting red lips. "Maybe you're right."

"Do you want me, Kyle?"

Her words stirred the fire in his groin, but he held back. "I think you know the answer to that." He moved closer, drawn to her despite his determination to keep his distance. "But that's not the real question, is it?"

She tilted her head slightly, obviously considering his words. "No, I guess not."

"Can you do this, Jenny? Can *we* do this? Can we make love tonight, and when this is all over, go our separate ways again?"

He heard her sharp intake of breath.

Taking a step closer, he wished he could lie, but knowing—this time, at least—she needed to hear the truth. "We live in separate worlds, Jen. Nothing's going to change. You know that, don't you?"

"Yes."

"Tell me no, Jenny. For both our sakes."

"I don't know if I can."

The silence stretched between them, long, uncertain, and filled with yearning. Finally, Jenny turned and crossed back to the other side of the room, stopping again at the bedroom doorway before once again facing him. "Make love to me, Kyle."

Kyle released the breath he hadn't realized he'd been holding and took a step forward.

SEVEN

Jenny watched as Kyle crossed the room to her, slowly, a stranger in black leather and denim. The only man she'd ever loved.

She should stop this. Now. Before they carried it too far. Yet she couldn't. Not after having touched him again, felt his lips on hers. Whatever else existed between them, there was this. This intense physical need for each other that no one else could satisfy.

He halted in front of her—perhaps giving her one last chance to change her mind. Instead, she met his gaze and backed into the bedroom. Kyle followed, matching her step for step, close enough this time that she could see the fire building in his eyes. She realized suddenly that she was no longer playing with a lit match, but a raging bonfire, and chances were she'd get burned. She didn't care.

Right now, she wanted him more than she feared an eternity of flames.

Her legs bumped up against the side of the oversize bed, startling her, and she reached for him to keep from falling. For a moment, two maybe, while her hand stilled on the hard muscles of his forearm, neither of them moved. It seemed to Jenny like neither of them breathed. Then he caught at her waist, hauling her against him with a fierceness that surprised her, while her arms found their way around his neck. And his mouth, his wonderfully wicked mouth, made claim to hers in a kiss that demanded she respond.

In that moment, all her questions and fears fled in the onslaught of her desire for him, in her need to make love with him once again. She was in his arms. *This* was where she belonged. And nothing else mattered.

He moved his hands up her back and down again to grip her bottom and bring her tighter against the hard front of him. Slivers of desire rippled through her, and she clung to his neck and shoulders, desperate for more.

Moaning, she tore her mouth from his. "Love me, Kyle, please love me."

"Ah, Jenny." He nipped at her mouth, bringing a soft moan to her lips. "How could I not?"

He grabbed her shirt and drew it up and over her head. Cool air teased her feverish skin, but it did little to temper the raging heat created by his hands. He released the front clasp of her bra and let it drop to the floor. Then, cupping her breasts, he brought her nipples to hard, aching points with his thumbs.

"God, how I've missed you," he sighed.

Jenny moaned again, the pleasure exquisite, as he stoked the fire inside her. Only Kyle could make her feel this way. No one else. Living without him had been pure hell; loving without him impossible.

Wanting to touch him as he touched her, she pushed his vest off his shoulders and let it fall to the floor. But Kyle beat her to his shirt, pulling it off and flinging it aside in one fluid motion. Almost instantly, her hands found his bare chest, and for a moment, she lost herself in the feel of warm skin and hard, tight muscle.

Kyle stood for a moment, letting her explore, while each stroke of her wonderfully long fingers tested his control. He'd never had much willpower where Jenny was concerned. Not before, and certainly not now. Still, he held on, wanting this time between them to last.

Then she found his nipples and lifted her warm honey eyes to his. It was the last straw, and he lost his battle with patience. Pushing her down onto the bed, he followed her, closing his mouth over one tantalizing breast while his hands worked at the front of her jeans.

Jenny arched into him, urging him on. But he couldn't get her stripped fast enough. Not for either of them. And there were the boots to contend with as well. She tried to help, fumbling with snaps and zippers while he pulled off her boots. Then their hands collided as he grabbed the denim and peeled it down her long, slender legs. The slip of silky underwear followed, until he finally had her where she belonged. Beneath him, naked and eager.

He kissed her, long and deep, the taste of her as addictive as the finest wine. His hands explored, tested, first the hardened tips of her nipples, then the sweet, silky moisture between her thighs. As his fingers delved deeper, she whimpered against his mouth, and he knew neither of them could wait any longer. Pulling back, he rose up on his knees and unfastened his jeans.

"Hurry," she said, her hands once again colliding with his as together they yanked his jeans down past his hips.

Moving between her thighs, he pushed her knees apart and bridged her with his arms. She met him halfway, her hands on his shoulders pulling him down, her hips arching to meet his as he thrust into her. And like a flash fire, it ignited them both, shattering his heart into bits and pieces he knew he'd never put together again.

Jenny lay for long minutes, wishing they could remain like this forever, joined in the most elemental of ways. There was a simplicity to it, a certain honesty in making love without thought or care about their past or future. And she wasn't going to ruin this night by thinking of either.

Then Kyle shifted his weight, rising on his elbows to smile down at her. "I must be heavy."

She stroked the hair that curled damply against his forehead. "Never."

He grinned and looked down at their joined hips. "You didn't even let me take off my jeans."

Laughter bubbled inside her, and she arched her hips against his, feeling him stir to life again. "Are you complaining?"

Kyle groaned and touched her lips with his. "Not in this lifetime."

"Then maybe we should try again." Tightening her hold around his neck, she traced his lips with her tongue. "Just to make sure we got it right."

Kyle laughed and shifted away from her. "Hold that thought."

Sitting on the edge of the bed, he pulled a small flat gun from one of his boots and set it on the dresser. For a moment, it brought her back to reality, forcing her to remember who they were and why they were there. Then he kicked off his boots, shucked his jeans and came back to her. And when his hands touched her again, she forgot the gun and tomorrow and the circumstances that had brought them back together.

He nuzzled her neck, sending shivers down her spine, before slipping back inside her. "This time we're going to go slowly."

He kept his promise, filling the too-short hours of the night with gentle hands and soft murmurs. He caressed, teased, and loved her until she thought her body could take no more. Then he started all over again, bringing her to the brink again and again, until finally they both collapsed, satiated.

Later, she lay in his arms, lingering on the edges of sleep, her mind drifting through the maze of emotions making love to Kyle had resurrected.

She'd thought she knew the cost of her dreams.

Losing Kyle had been a high price to pay, but she'd told herself that someday she'd forget him. She'd meet someone new and fall in love again. She'd marry, have children, and build the kind of family she'd never had.

For five years she'd been lying to herself.

The price of her dream was so much higher.

Oh, she could still have a family. If she forgot about love or honesty. If she married a man she didn't love. A man who could never be Kyle.

Kyle opened his eyes.

He and Jenny had fallen asleep just before dawn. Now, early-morning light streamed through the windows. Something had awakened him. Years of experience kept him motionless just long enough to identify the low hum of an approaching bike.

He rolled from the bed and grabbed his jeans.

"What is it?" Jenny whispered, rising halfway, holding a sheet in front of her.

"Get dressed." Kyle pulled on his jeans and snatched the Beretta from the dresser. "We've got company."

"Kyle?"

He'd frightened her, but that couldn't be helped now. "It might be nothing, but get dressed anyway. Quickly." He opened the bedroom door and moved into the outer room.

The bike drew nearer: a Harley by the sound of it. He couldn't imagine Casale's men announcing their arrival, or showing up in anything less than a fleet of limousines. Unless it was meant to throw him off. Which was entirely possible. One thing the last forty-eight hours had taught him, was not to underestimate Vittorio Casale.

Keeping close to the wall, Kyle worked his way toward the front of the room. Then, with his back pressed against the door, he inched forward just enough to peer through the window.

Outside everything was quiet. Except for the continued low throb of the approaching bike. Kyle rested his gun on the edge of the window, adrenaline racing through his system.

Then Samson pulled into the front yard on his oversize chopper.

Kyle released his breath and eased the gun back down to his side. Still, he remained behind the door. He trusted Samson with his life, but he wasn't taking any chances with Jenny's. He'd made that mistake in the cabin outside Atlanta, and she'd almost paid the price.

Samson shut down his bike, climbed off and glanced around. Then he headed for the front door and knocked, as if the cabin didn't belong to him. "Munroe?"

"You alone?" Kyle asked, moving away from the door to stand against the wall alongside it.

"Yeah. I'm alone."

Kyle opened the door just enough for the big man to enter.

Taking one look at the automatic in Kyle's hand, Samson frowned. "I take it you were expecting someone else?"

Kyle stuffed the weapon into the waistband of his jeans. "Just a precaution. What are you doing here?"

"I've got a message for you. From DeMitri."

"He's alive?"

Both men turned to see Jenny standing in the bedroom doorway, fully dressed in jeans and one of Kyle's shirts.

"Yes, ma'am," Samson answered. "I just talked to him before heading out here." To Kyle, he added, "You need to contact this DeMitri fella right away." Reaching into his back pocket, he pulled out a single piece of paper. "Says he'll be at this number for the next hour. That was"—he checked his watch—"fifteen minutes ago."

Kyle took the paper and glanced at it. Then he looked at Jenny. "Samson, stay with her while I take care of this."

"No." She moved to Kyle's side. "Why can't you make the call from here?"

He steeled himself against her fear. "I can't risk anyone tracing the call."

"Then take me with you."

"The more you stay out of sight, the safer you'll be." Before he could stop himself, he brought a hand up to caress the silky skin of her cheek. "You'll be safe here. Samson's a good man."

She blinked back her tears and turned her lips into his hand. A moment was all he allowed himself—a moment to cradle her face and wish for a lifetime. Then he backed away from her. Quickly. Before he could change his mind. And looked to Samson.

"Don't worry," the other man said. "I'll take care of her."

"I need an hour." Kyle moved toward the door. "If I'm not back by then—"

"There's a bike trail behind the cabin. I'll get her out."

"Thanks, my friend." Kyle held out his hand, and Samson grasped it.

"Go ahead, get out of here."

With one last glance at Jenny, Kyle turned and headed out the door.

Jenny followed him to the door, closing it behind him and then going to stand at the window and watch him pull out of the yard. It reminded her of the last time he'd left her—five years ago. Everything about that day had been different—though in some ways, it felt the same.

It had been autumn instead of spring, with winter hovering on the fringes of tomorrow. Kyle had worn the standard dark suit, not denim and leather, and had driven a four-door government-issued sedan instead of a black Harley.

And they'd decided to go their separate ways.

Actually, the decision had been made months earlier, before he'd found her the house and set up her new identity. But up until that last day she'd held hope close, needing him to change his mind and stay with her.

It all came back to her now, the bittersweet details of those last hours they had spent together, as if time had come full circle. The empty rooms with their new-house smells of wood and paint. The stiffness of the carpet as they made love one last time, their sighs echoing through the yet unfurnished rooms. Her tears, burning her eyes, as she begged him to stay. Then the hollowness of a house with too many rooms when he left.

And the chill.

Mostly the chill, like she felt now, rubbing her hands over her upper arms. She knew Kyle would return for her, had known it five years ago when she'd watched him drive away from her new Atlanta home. But like then, she knew that when he returned, it would be different between them. It wouldn't matter that they'd spent the night in each other's arms. The spell had been broken. He'd come back as a federal marshal rather than her lover, and she'd once again be just part of his job.

And she, once again, would be left to somehow deal with that.

"Jenny?"

She turned abruptly, realizing Samson had said her name more than once. "I'm sorry. What were you saying?"

"Coffee?" He lifted an obviously full pot off the stove. "It's fresh."

The aroma floated toward her, and she wondered how long she'd been standing there oblivious to everything but her own thoughts. Obviously long enough for Samson to brew coffee.

"That sounds great," she said, and turned her back on the window. Crossing the room, she took the cup he offered.

"Don't worry," he said. "Munroe's the best."

Jenny smiled tightly and sipped at the coffee. "So he keeps telling me."

"Believe him."

Then she realized how Kyle knew this man. "You're in the Federal Witness Protection Program, aren't you? One of Kyle's witnesses."

Samson smiled broadly, apparently pleased with the distinction. "One of his first."

She wondered why she hadn't thought of it before. It explained so much. "How long has it been?"

"Nearly eight years. Of course, I'm breaking the rules telling you about it, but since you're Munroe's woman . . ." He shrugged and let his voice trail off.

"We aren't . . ." she started, and then stopped

herself. She could tell from his expression that Samson wouldn't believe her denial. Besides, all he had to do was take a look at the mess she and Kyle had made of his bed to know how they'd spent the night.

"For Munroe, hiding someone like you is easy," Samson said. "But me?" He let out one short burst of laughter. "Try hiding a giant."

The man's humor was infectious, and Jenny couldn't help but return his smile. "I take it you weren't always a bartender."

"The first rule of disappearing is to become someone else. That's what I did. With Munroe's help. He found a place I fit, more than the place I left. So you see, I owe the man more than my life. I owe him my happiness."

Jenny didn't know what to say. There were questions she could ask, about Samson's former life or the event that had sent him into hiding. But she didn't. He'd already told her too much. The rest of his secrets would remain his.

Besides, he'd made her think of other things, of Kyle and the job he performed, and a flush of shame swept through her.

On one level, she'd always known about the people Kyle protected. Yet, she'd never really thought about it, never considered the lives he saved and put back together. Instead, she'd viewed his work as a problem, the main force that kept them apart.

Now, across from her sat a giant of a man; a

man who from all outward appearances could handle anything. Yet someone wanted him dead. Someone dangerous. And Kyle had been his salvation. He'd not only given Samson a chance at survival, he'd given Samson a life.

She'd been blind and selfish. And though she knew it meant losing him, she was beginning to understand that she could never take Kyle away from all the future Samsons in his life.

The phone rang five times.

Kyle was considering hanging up when someone finally picked up, and a voice on the other end said, "DeMitri."

Kyle breathed a sigh of relief. "I expected to hear from you yesterday."

"Sorry, things have gotten a little complicated."

"Yeah? Well, what else is new?" Kyle scanned the convenience store parking lot where he'd made the call. Everything seemed quiet. "You okay? What about Cross and the man Billy sliced up?"

"Cross took a bullet in the shoulder, but he'll be fine. Billy's in custody, and the officer he cut will make it."

Kyle nodded, glad the other man couldn't see his relief. They all knew the risks inherent in their job, and Kyle second-guessing his decisions because of his concern over them could be considered a weakness.

"Look," DeMitri said, "we don't have much

time. This call might be traced. Is Miss Brooks there?"

Kyle hesitated a second before answering. "She's safe."

"With you?"

"What's this about, DeMitri?"

Kyle could hear the other man's hesitation through the phone line. "We got a problem, Munroe."

EIGHT

Kyle knew it was a trap.

Pushing the bike to its limit, he counted the seconds as the tires ate the asphalt. He was close to the time limit he'd set for returning to the cabin, and he knew Samson would flee with Jenny if Kyle was so much as a minute late.

Meanwhile, every instinct he possessed screamed at him to forget about the call to DeMitri and take Jenny as far away as possible. The two of them could disappear, and no one would ever find them. Then they could forget all about Casale and her father, and their games of justice and intrigue. Kyle and Jenny would be out of it.

Yet, he knew they couldn't run.

Though the why of it escaped him at the moment. Somehow his duty had gotten all mixed up between wanting to protect Jenny, and just plain wanting her. His job was to safeguard the innocent.

Nothing personal. Yet, it had become personal, very personal. In just forty-eight short hours Jenny had reclaimed the piece of his soul he thought he'd locked away forever. And if he continued on his current course, he would no longer know who or what he was protecting. Jenny? His job? Or a federal appellate judge who cared more about his perceived justice than his only daughter.

Still, Kyle knew he could no longer keep Jenny safe. Not indefinitely and not under these circumstances. Not without forcing her to give up everything she loved. She'd be running the rest of her life, with no chance for the normalcy she craved.

He couldn't do that to her.

That's why he couldn't ignore DeMitri's information and make a run for it. That's why, even though he knew it was a trap, he had to take Jenny back to Washington.

He came up on the cutoff to Samson's place and slowed just enough to make the turn without ditching the bike. Unfortunately, the rough, unpaved surface checked his speed, and he cursed Samson the whole way for living so far off the main road.

Finally, he skidded to a stop in front of the cabin with barely five minutes to spare.

Jenny met him at the door, and his resolve to do the right thing weakened. He wanted to drag her into his arms and carry her off. He knew she'd go with him, and he'd explain later what she'd given up. Instead, he steeled himself against the temptation and brushed past her.

He saw the hurt on her face and the disapproval on Samson's. He ignored both. "Get ready, Jenny. We're heading back to Washington."

"Washington?" Shock replaced hurt, and she followed him across the room, grabbing his arm and forcing him to look at her. "Why? What's wrong?"

He couldn't let her get to him, change what he had to do. Pulling away from her, he started checking the contents of his duffel bag. "I'm taking you to your father."

"Why?" she asked, anxiety and confusion lacing her voice. "What's going on?"

"Your father thinks Casale has succeeded in taking you hostage."

"But how?"

He stopped and looked at her then. He couldn't help himself. Her strength drew him. The resolve he heard in her voice, her determination not to succumb to fear. "Casale sent him some pictures of you. And a tape of your voice." He paused, fighting the frustration and anger swelling within him. She didn't deserve this. "Lord knows where he got either, but since no one has seen you since we left the safe house in Georgia, your father's convinced you're in Casale's tender loving care."

She seized his arm again, tighter this time. "But you told him that's not right, didn't you?"

"I told DeMitri. But your father's not going to believe anything until he hears it from you."

"So, let's call him. I'll tell him I'm with you."

She moved toward the phone and grabbed the receiver.

Kyle stopped her before she could lift it from its cradle. "We'll try, but not from here. Your father's phone will be tapped, and we can't take the chance they'll trace the call back here."

"Forget about me, Munroe," Samson said. "Go ahead. Make your call, Jenny."

"No." Kyle turned on the bigger man, who'd moved up behind him. "I won't risk it. I won't sacrifice one of you for the other."

For a long, breathless moment Samson didn't budge, glaring at Kyle as if ready to challenge him. Kyle held his ground, knowing he was right and willing Samson to do the same. "Back off, Samson. This is no concern of yours."

Finally, Samson nodded, stepped back and crossed the room to stand by the front windows.

Kyle released his breath and turned back to Jenny. "We'll try to call from the road, but I doubt we'll get through. Casale doesn't want you contacting your father."

"He can do that? Keep me from getting through?"

"I don't know, Jen." Kyle led her away from the phone. "But at this point I wouldn't put anything past him."

"But why?" she said, the fear finally creeping into her voice. "What does Casale have to gain at this point? My father's a judge, not a witness. He can't help Philip Casale. After these threats, he'll probably be forced to step down, and someone else will try the case. Or, if he happens to convince the court that he can be impartial, every decision he makes will be so closely scrutinized that there would be no way he could let Philip off."

"It's no longer about Philip." Kyle eased her into a chair and, pulling up another, sat in front of her and took her hands. "Casale is sending a message. Not only to your father but to anyone who dares oppose him."

Her eyes widened, realization and then shock claiming her features. "He's going to make an example of me?"

Kyle wished he could say she was wrong, or give her some platitude about everything turning out okay. He couldn't do either. The time for lies and half-truths was over. Jenny needed to understand what was at stake.

"In Casale's mind," he started, keeping a firm grip on her hands, "your father's first mistake was trying to protect you by calling in federal marshals. If he'd kept the threat against you a secret, you would have been safe. You'd have been watched, but not touched, until Philip won his appeal. Then it would have been over."

"But that's not my father's way."

"No." Kyle softened his voice. "It's not. And the minute he came to us, Casale had no choice but to make a move against you. Then he lets your father know you're still alive, and again, in Casale's mind, there's still a chance Philip will walk."

"But that's not what would happen. Philip—"

"It doesn't matter," Kyle said, cutting her off. She was thinking rationally and forgetting that Casale wouldn't do the same. "How your father lets Philip walk is of no concern to Casale. He would consider it your father's problem."

"And if Philip's appeal is denied?" Jenny pulled away from him and stood. "Or Father is pulled from the case?"

"The results are the same." Kyle started to follow her but stopped himself, seeing that she needed to hear this without the comfort of his arms. "Casale kills you, considering it a child for a child. Then the next judge who comes up against him thinks twice."

Jenny wrapped her arms around her middle, visibly shaken. "But why go back then?"

Kyle hesitated, fighting the impulse to tell her there was no reason they *should* go back. "That has to be your decision. But there are a couple of things you need to consider."

She didn't ask, but he could see the questions on her face.

"If we don't go to Washington," he said, "it'll never end. There will be no turning back. No changing our minds."

"It's not much of an option, is it?"

"If it's your only choice"—Kyle glanced at Samson—"it's a way to stay alive."

"You said there were two things. What's the other?"

"If we run"—he paused, wishing he could forget this part—"you won't be the last person Casale goes after."

Jenny hesitated, and Kyle found himself again hoping she'd decide to forget Casale and her father.

"Okay," she said. "You're right. What do you want me to do?"

Disappointment washed over him, though he knew she'd made the right decision. Closing the distance between them, he gripped her upper arms. "I can't protect you until I know how Casale got his information. We need to get him out in the open, force his hand and take him down."

"And I'm the bait."

Kyle hesitated, wishing there were another way. "I'm afraid so."

It took them about twenty minutes to get on the road.

Twenty minutes of strained silence, while Jenny got ready in the bedroom and Kyle checked his gear once again. Samson went outside to his bike and returned carrying something wrapped in what looked like a pink towel. Then he stood by the window, as big and dark and thunderous as an approaching storm. Kyle knew better than to try to explain himself to the other man—Samson's thoughts on the subject were clear without any more unpleasant words between them.

When Jenny came back out, she'd dressed as she

had the day before, in jeans, boots, and the skimpy white top. She'd reapplied the heavy makeup and carried the leather jacket over one arm.

Then Samson turned from the window and handed her the pink bundle. "Delilah sent this to you."

Jenny smiled awkwardly and glanced at Kyle before unwrapping it. Her smile faded. Inside was a small, lightweight pocket Colt automatic in a holster. Kyle wished he'd thought of it.

"Oh, Samson," she said, pushing the Colt back into the big man's hands. "I appreciate the thought, but I can't take this. I'm not comfortable with guns."

"It's not a matter of comfort. Delilah said you might need it." He glanced at Kyle. "I tend to agree."

"But—"

"It's perfect," Kyle interrupted, taking the gun from Jenny's hand. "Sit down and take off your boot."

"My boot?"

"This is an ankle holster. The gun will fit snugly inside your boot, and no one will know you're carrying it."

Jenny put up token protests while Kyle showed her the gun and how the holster conformed securely to her ankle. But in the end, she wore it. Maybe because she'd begun to realize just how precarious their position had become.

Then as they started to leave, Kyle said to Samson, "Thanks for everything. There shouldn't be any problems, but if there are . . ."

"I have a local contact."

Kyle nodded, knowing a local federal marshal had been assigned to Samson shortly after Kyle had placed him.

"Okay, then." He didn't know what else to say, so he started to walk away, but Samson's big hand on his shoulder stopped him. He turned and met the other man's gaze, seeing the warning in his eyes.

"Don't you hurt her, Munroe."

"It's my job to protect her, Samson."

"I've no doubt you'll do that. From this Casale fella anyway. But who's going to protect her from you?"

It was a question that rattled around in Kyle's mind for the rest of the morning. Five years ago he'd hurt Jenny when he refused to move to Atlanta with her. On the surface, it had looked like her fault. She'd been the one to move away and ask him to give up his career. But there had been more to it than that, more than he'd ever told her.

Again fate had brought them together, possibly giving him another chance. Only he couldn't see how it would end. How could he keep from hurting her this time?

One negative thing about traveling by motorcycle, Jenny decided, was since it was too loud to talk, it gave you too much time to think. Which under the current circumstances, wasn't necessarily a good thing.

The thought of returning to Washington frightened her. Yet she couldn't entertain the alternative—going into hiding for the rest of her life. If that was even a possibility anymore with Casale seeming to know every step they took. She'd given up her identity once before when she moved to Atlanta to lead a quiet life away from her father. But it had been her choice, and she'd always had the option of returning. As Kyle had pointed out, if she went into hiding now, there would be no turning back.

Which brought her thoughts to Kyle.

She'd been right earlier when she'd watched him leave the cabin to call DeMitri. When he'd returned, things had been different. *He'd* been different. He'd returned to the role of protector, keeping his distance even as he held her hands to comfort her. And though she'd expected it, his withdrawal had been a direct blow to her heart. There was nothing left but a dull ache inside her, overriding her fear of Casale.

Yet, she didn't regret their night together. She'd tuck away the memories of those hours, save them for after Kyle and she went their separate ways. Then she'd pull them out and savor every moment. It wasn't much, but it would have to do.

For now, though, she just needed to get through this. To face Vittorio Casale and come out of it alive. Only then could she try to rebuild her life. Alone.

They rode east as the sun crept toward noon, stopping only once for gas and to try and contact her father. As Kyle had warned, the call didn't go through. Then, because he said they needed to move on, they bought juice and stale prewrapped sandwiches to eat on the way. Back on the road, they headed toward her father and his enemies.

That's why it surprised her when Kyle pulled off the road again a couple of hours later. He picked a combination gas station, convenience store, and diner, with a parking lot lined with eighteen-wheelers, RV's, and travel trailers. She considered questioning him as he shut down the engine in front of the restaurant, but decided against it. She was tired and hungry. If Kyle wanted to change his mind about stopping to eat, she was all for it.

Inside the diner, a row of booths ran along the windows, a counter fronted the kitchen directly facing the door, and a scattering of tables sat in between.

Kyle led her to the last booth, taking the far side where he sat with his back to the wall. They hardly spoke as they surveyed the menus and ordered. There really wasn't much else to say. At the cabin they'd discussed the situation with Casale at length. As for addressing more personal topics, she figured neither of them were particularly anxious to start.

Then Kyle surprised her again by reaching across the table and covering her hands with his. "Jenny, look at me," he said. "And don't turn around."

The tone of his voice frightened her, but she did as he instructed, keeping her eyes steady. "What's wrong?"

He tightened his hold on her hands. "We're being followed."

It took a moment, but she reined in her fear, forcing it down to a manageable level. Kyle must have sensed she'd regained control, because he released her hands just as the waitress appeared with coffee.

"Just act normal," he said as she left. Picking up one of the cups, he sipped at the coffee. "They've been trailing us for most of the morning. But I don't think they know I've spotted them."

Jenny wrapped her hands around her own cup, needing to hold on to something now that Kyle had withdrawn his hands. "Where are they?"

"First booth near the door."

It was a struggle not to turn and look for herself. "Maybe it's a coincidence." Although she knew it was too much to hope for.

Kyle shrugged. "Maybe."

"But you don't think so."

"I'm not taking any chances."

"How did they find us?"

Frustration and another emotion she couldn't

name crossed his features. "The same way they knew about your place and the safe house. Someone must have told them."

"Who?"

He paused, that wayward emotion surfacing. "DeMitri."

Jenny flinched. "I don't believe it."

"I don't want to believe it either." She recognized that second emotion now. Betrayal. The thought of DeMetri working for Casale would tear at Kyle. "There's no other explanation. He knew about the cabin in Georgia."

"So did Cross and the other officers from Atlanta."

"But DeMitri was the only one who had Samson's phone number. Using the department's computers, he must have cross-referenced it to get the location. Then sent men who followed Samson to the cabin and waited for us to move. Short of dumb luck, it's the only way they could have found us."

"And you don't believe in dumb luck."

"Do you?"

No, she couldn't say she did. But she didn't want to believe DeMitri had betrayed them either. Then she thought of something else. "What about my house?" she asked. "You said no one knew where I was in Atlanta. Not even DeMitri or Cross."

Kyle shook his head. "I don't know. That's the one thing that doesn't add up."

"So, it might *not* be DeMitri."

"There's one other thing," Kyle said. Jenny looked up at him, waiting for the final blow. "Somehow DeMitri survived the cabin the other night."

The waitress picked that moment to show up, placing full plates of food in front of them and filling their coffee. When she left, Jenny said, "Okay. Let's say DeMitri is behind all this. I assume you have a plan."

Kyle flashed her a brief, unexpected smile and picked up his fork. "Yeah, I do. But first, we eat." When she didn't respond immediately, he nodded toward her plate. "Go ahead."

Jenny had lost interest in eating, but she made a stab at it, taking a bite of her hamburger and toying with the fries.

"If they wanted to grab you," Kyle said, as if reading her thoughts, "they would have made a move by now. Probably when we stopped for gas a couple of hours ago."

"Gee, that makes me feel a whole lot better." She couldn't help the sarcasm. It was that or scream. "So, what *are* they doing following us then?"

"My guess is they're keeping an eye on us. Casale knows we're heading back to Washington." Again that quick smile, and Jenny realized that on some level Kyle was enjoying this—the challenge of outsmarting an opponent and taking a criminal down. "Hell, he's counting on it. Then, when we get closer, he'll make his move."

"So," she said again. "What do we do?"

"We lose them."

"Kyle . . ." She put a warning in her voice, wanting more than Kyle's usual terse explanation.

"Okay. After we eat, you head for the ladies' room. But instead of going inside, I want you to duck into the kitchen. There's a door at the end of the hallway. Then walk out the back way."

"And if someone stops me and asks what I'm doing there?"

"Be creative. Tell them you're trying to ditch your boyfriend or something." He grinned. "They'll take one look at me and believe it."

Jenny rolled her eyes, though she guessed he was right. One look at this man and any sensible woman would run. Unfortunately she wasn't feeling very sensible at the moment. Right now she wanted to beg Kyle to let her stay with him. Where she felt safe.

"But chances are," Kyle continued, "no one will say a word. Just walk into the kitchen and out the back door like you belong. Then wait for me outside. Stay behind the restaurant and keep out of sight."

"And what are you going to do?"

"I'm going out the front. If I'm right, one of them will follow me and the other will stay behind waiting for you. They might even get creative themselves and decide now is as good a time as any to grab you."

"Great."

They continued eating in silence. Somehow Jenny managed to force down part of her hamburger, while struggling to repress her fear. Kyle would tell her that fear was her deadliest enemy. Keep calm, he'd say, and use your head. It sounded so easy. When in reality, nothing had ever been more difficult.

"You ready?"

His question startled her out of her thoughts, but she managed a quick nod. "As ready as I'm going to be."

"Remember—"

"I know, out the back door and wait for you."

"That's my girl. Now smile."

She forced a smile past the fear prickling along her insides and slid out of the booth before she could change her mind. She headed for the short hall leading to the rest rooms, feeling as if every eye in the place followed her. She counted her steps, surprised when it seemed to take hours to cross such a short space.

Once in the hallway, she picked up her pace, hurrying through the door that led into the kitchen. And stopped, waiting for someone to challenge her.

No one even noticed her.

Jenny shook her head, almost smiling that Kyle had been right once again, and worked her way through the maze of stainless steel kitchen equipment to the back door.

Outside, she took a deep breath and moved away from the rear entrance. Now, all she had to do was wait for Kyle and hope his streak of being right held.

NINE

Kyle waited until Jenny had time to get out the back door before he dropped a few dollars on the table, picked up the check and slid from the booth. Making his way toward the cashier, he passed the men he suspected of following them.

Casale was getting careless.

Kyle had first spotted these two shortly after leaving Samson's cabin over four hours ago. Since he'd been on a back road, avoiding the main highway, he'd have been an idiot to miss them.

Seeing them up close confirmed it.

They were about as subtle as twin bulls after a red flag: big, dumb, and clumsy. They were the kind of men who took orders without question—as long as those orders weren't too complicated—and got their jollies inflicting pain. Not exactly the pros Kyle would have expected the crime lord to send after him and Jenny.

Of course, sending the big dumb ones in first might be part of Casale's plan. He could be trying to lull Kyle into a sense of security.

Well, it wasn't going to work.

After paying his check, Kyle walked outside and headed for the bike, smiling to himself as one of the twins came out as well.

Kyle figured he had about ten minutes. Ten minutes to dispatch twin number one and get Jenny out of there before twin number two went looking for her. He spent a couple of those minutes making a few unneeded adjustments to the Harley's engine. Then, playing his role to the hilt, he looked toward the ladies' room inside, shook his head and glanced at his watch. With an exaggerated sigh, he hoisted his bag over his shoulder and started toward the convenience store.

Inside, he browsed. As he'd hoped, the other man came in a few moments later. By that time Kyle had picked up a couple of small items someone traveling on a motorcycle might carry and headed for the cashier. He paid for his selections and asked for the key to the men's room outside.

The clerk handed over the key with Kyle's change.

Kyle walked back outside, only this time, he turned right and rounded the corner of the store. Instead of going into the men's room, he ducked behind a nearby Dumpster and pulled his automatic from the waistband at the small of his back.

And waited.

A minute passed. Two. And Kyle began to wonder if he'd miscalculated. Suddenly the thought of Jenny alone, waiting behind the diner seemed terribly risky. If his plan didn't work, and something happened to her . . .

No!

He needed to stop second-guessing himself because of his feelings for Jenny. He'd read those men right, knew one of them would come looking for him any moment. He needed to stay put just a little longer. Sure enough, a couple of seconds later his man ambled around the corner and stopped in front of the men's room.

"Hey, buddy," Kyle said, stepping from behind the Dumpster and holding up the key in his left hand. "You looking for this?"

The man turned, surprise flickering across his features, and reached inside his jacket . . .

A moment too late.

Kyle closed the distance between them, shielding his gun hand with his body, and brought the 9 mm Beretta level with the other man's gut. "Not a good idea, friend."

"Who *the hell* are you?"

"Oh, I think you know the answer to that one. Here"—Kyle tossed him the key—"let's go inside and talk about it."

"Like hell," he balked. "You ain't gonna shoot me."

"Won't I?" Kyle moved in closer, letting the

barrel of the Beretta press against the man's soft belly. "Why's that?"

The man sucked in his breath but glared at Kyle. "You're a cop. And cops don't go around shooting folks."

"That's where you're wrong, friend." Kyle nudged his big belly with the Beretta. "I ain't no cop. I'm a federal officer, and you"—he pressed the gun harder—"are interfering with my duties. As long as I fill out the right paperwork, no one's going to ask any questions if you turn up dead. So what will it be? Makes no difference to me."

The man hesitated, emotions flitting across his features. Kyle bit back his impatience, knowing it was only a matter of time before someone rounded the corner and found the two of them. Finally, the man turned and opened the rest room door.

"Smart move." Kyle shoved him inside and followed, closing and locking the door behind them. He was running out of time. No telling how long this man's other half would sit in the diner before he went searching for Jenny.

"Okay," Kyle said, motioning toward the sink. "On the floor."

"The friggin' floor's filthy."

Kyle lifted his gun a little higher. "It'll be a whole lot messier if you don't do what I tell you."

The man shot him a murderous look but got down on the floor. Kyle reached into his bag and produced his handcuffs. Tossing them to the man, he said, "Put these on and attach it to that drain-pipe."

"Hey, man, it stinks in here."

"That it does." Kyle grabbed a rag he'd stuffed in his back pocket after fiddling with the bike. "Open up."

"Go to hell."

Kyle brought the automatic up and pressed it against the man's forehead. "It sure would be a bitch to fill out all that paperwork."

The man opened his mouth, and Kyle stuffed it with the rag.

"There you go," Kyle said, stepping back to survey his handiwork. "Don't worry, I'm sure someone will find you sooner or later." He started for the door, stopping with his hand on the handle, and turned. "Just in case you're wondering," he said, "I *would* have shot you."

Outside, he tossed the key into a nearby gully and headed around back to get Jenny.

Jenny paced behind the diner.

What was taking Kyle so long? Glancing at her watch for the tenth time in as many minutes, she told herself to be patient. Something she'd never been very good at. Especially when she could imagine any number of scenarios, all of them ending badly with Kyle hurt or needing help, while she hid out behind this building.

She couldn't wait forever. If he didn't show up

soon, she'd go looking for him, despite his instructions to the contrary. After all, he wasn't invincible. Another five minutes, she decided, and . . .

A stranger stepped around the corner of the building, and Jenny stopped cold. She knew without being told that this was one of the men following her and Kyle, and the realization sent slivers of fear slipping down her spine.

"You lost?" he asked, walking toward her in easy, unhurried steps.

She thought to run, but somehow the message never reached her legs. "No, I'm . . ." *Think fast, Jenny.* ". . . I was just getting some fresh air."

The man grinned, a wide, unpleasant expression that tightened the tendrils of fear reaching for her. "Great place for it." He glanced around at the overflowing Dumpster and stacks of soggy produce boxes. "Smells good too. Maybe you could use some company."

"Actually," she said, putting more bravado into her voice than she felt, "I was just getting ready to go in."

She started to step past him, but he grabbed her arm. "What's your hurry?"

"What do you think you're doing?" Even to her own ears, her voice sounded shrill. She tried to yank her arm from his grasp. "Let go of me."

"I've got a better idea. Why don't you come with me and I'll make sure you get lots of fresh air."

"No thank you."

He pulled a large lethal-looking gun from inside his jacket. "I insist."

Fear seized her, and Jenny ceased struggling.

That's when she spotted Kyle, over the other man's shoulder, keeping close to the wall as he closed the distance between them.

Bolstering her courage, Jenny looked Casale's man straight in the eyes and used her most haughty tone of voice. "Obviously, you don't know who I am. My father is a very powerful man. You *better* let go of me."

The man laughed. "Hey, lady. I don't give a damn who—"

He never got to finish his sentence. His grip on her arm went slack as he sank to the ground under Kyle's blow.

Relief washed through her fear, leaving only anger. "Where have you been?"

"No time for that now. Come on." Kyle grabbed her hand and half led, half pulled her back in the direction he'd come. When they reached the edge of the building, he stopped short and draped his arm around her shoulder. "Now, act normally."

"You mean like someone who didn't just get manhandled by a gorilla with a gun?"

He shot her a grin and squeezed her shoulder. "Exactly."

Jenny wasn't amused, but his arm felt good, reassuring, and shifting closer to him, she could almost forget the last few minutes. Almost. To Kyle this might all be business as usual, but she'd never get used to running and hiding, or facing men with weapons.

They started across the parking lot, and she realized they weren't heading toward the bike. "Where are we going?"

"To hitch a ride."

They'd reached the edge of the parking lot, with its space for oversize vehicles. There were several eighteen-wheelers, an RV, and a couple of trucks with trailers attached. Kyle led her to a good-size travel trailer hitched to a pickup truck.

"Okay," she said, afraid she knew the answer before she asked. "Now what?"

"Just watch." Releasing her, Kyle glanced around and then pulled a wire from his bag and started working on the lock. "Keep an eye out for me, will you? I'd hate to get busted for breaking and entering."

"That would be something," she said, though she did as he'd asked, turning her back to him and watching out for anyone who might notice Kyle picking the lock. "I can see the headlines now. Federal Marshal and judge's daughter caught using unsuspecting tourist's trailer as getaway vehicle."

"People don't ride in their trailers," Kyle said, obviously ignoring her sarcasm. "It's not safe."

"So, of course, that's exactly what we're going to do. Ride in a trailer. Makes sense to me."

"For us it's safer than continuing on the bike until Casale figures we're close enough to Washington to grab you."

"In case you hadn't noticed, someone already tried to *grab* me."

"My point exactly. Get in." He'd gotten the door open and ushered her into the trailer. "Stay down," he added, "below the windows." He closed the door behind them and locked it again.

The inside was bigger than she'd expected, roomy almost. The front end consisted of a kitchen and sitting area, complete with sink, stove, minifridge, and eating nook. Down the middle stretched a long benchlike couch, with built-in cabinets above and below. On the other side were more doors and cabinets. In the back, a set of full-size bunk beds spread across the entire width.

It was neat and homey all at the same time, and Jenny felt like an intruder. "I don't like this, Kyle. What if the owners decide to come in before leaving?"

"We're going to hope that doesn't happen. But just in case"—he opened a door to a bathroom barely large enough for one full-size adult—"we're going to get out of sight."

"Kyle, it's awfully small." She knew how he felt about tight spaces.

"I'll be fine. There's plenty of light. Besides, it's the last place they'll look."

Too overwhelmed to argue or even ask any more questions, Jenny stepped inside. Kyle squeezed in behind her, closing the door just as she heard approaching voices. She held her breath, and Kyle wrapped his arms around her, eliminating what little space remained between them. Resting her head against his chest, she listened to the steady rhythm of his heart and tried not to dwell on the people outside.

She didn't think she could handle another confrontation today. Who knew what would happen if the owners of this trailer discovered them? She and Kyle could be arrested, or worse yet, they could run into the men who'd followed them. She didn't want to draw innocent bystanders into her problems.

Suddenly, the trailer began to move, a slow rocking at first, as she imagined the truck starting up and pulling out of the parking lot. After a few minutes they picked up speed and were soon moving along at a good clip.

"It looks like we got lucky," Kyle said.

Jenny nodded, too relieved to speak.

"Are you all right?" he asked, his voice a low, husky whisper. "He didn't hurt you, did he?"

"No," she managed. *Not physically*.

Kyle tightened his hold on her. "I'm sorry, Jen, so sorry it took me so long."

Now that they were out of immediate danger, tears of fear and relief swelled inside her. She'd been holding them back since Kyle had come to her rescue. Now they caught in her throat. She fought them. The last thing he needed was a blubbering woman on his hands. Yet, twice now one of Casale's men had come close to kidnapping her. Twice she'd seen her own death within touching distance. She'd never been more frightened in her life.

Yet, that wasn't the worst part.

The worst part was being held by Kyle again, loving the feel of his arms and knowing that it couldn't last. She didn't belong in his crazy, dangerous world. And they both knew it. He would be here only as long as she needed protection. No longer. When it was all over he'd walk away, and she . . .

Grabbing his vest in both hands, Jenny pressed her forehead against his chest and let the tears flow.

Kyle held her close, letting her cry.

He didn't know what else to do. Especially since he wasn't feeling too steady himself. When he'd rounded that corner back at the truck stop and seen Casale's man with his hands on her, it had taken all his training and discipline to keep from tearing the man apart limb from limb. Somehow he'd managed to control himself, and Jenny was safe.

Yet, the danger loomed ever stronger and more deadly as they drew closer to Washington. He wished he could change things, make all of this go away for her. Unfortunately, he knew only one way to help her. And that meant facing things straight on.

Finally, her tears subsided, and she lifted her head and looked up at him, a shaky smile on her tearstained face. "I guess I broke my promise."

"What promise is that?"

"Not to fall apart on you again."

Kyle smiled and grabbed a tissue from the dispenser built into the stainless steel sink. "Is that what you just did?" He wiped her damp cheeks. "All I saw were a few cathartic tears. And if I weren't a man," he teased, "I might have joined you."

Jenny laughed and Kyle thought he'd never heard a lovelier sound. Before he could stop himself, he bent to catch it, feathering his lips against hers before deepening the kiss.

He kept it gentle, moving his hands to cradle her face, relishing the sweet confirmation of life he found in her silky mouth. He'd come so close to losing her, he needed this taste, this one moment when he could push all the ugliness aside.

Reluctantly, he broke the kiss. "Feel better?"

Her lips inched upward. "Much. Maybe I should cry more often."

Kyle matched her smile, amazed at her strength and resiliency. So much had happened to her in the last few days, with no time for her to adjust to any of it. Yet, after one good cry, she could grin and tease him.

So much for his resolve to keep his distance. It had lasted all of five hours. But then his ability to resist Jenny had always been close to nil.

"Think maybe we should go to the outer room?" he asked. "It might be a bit more comfortable."

"Oh, I don't know." Her smile turned impish, and she slipped her hands under his vest, running elegant fingers across his chest. "It's kind of cozy in here."

"Too cozy." Kyle claimed her wrists and held her wandering hands away from him. "And you're entirely too tempting."

"Come on. . . ." Jenny rose on her tiptoes and pressed her lips to the hollow of his throat. "It reminds me of the bus."

"The bus?"

She pulled back. "Don't tell me you forgot about the bus. At the camp where I was a counselor that first summer."

"This is nothing like that school bus. We had the whole backseat to spread out on."

"Yes, but it was deliciously wicked."

"You"—he nipped at her mouth—"are deliciously wicked." Releasing her hands, he slid his own down to her bottom and pulled her against him so she could feel just how wicked. "And I'm not immune. But the back of that bus was risky and irresponsible. Just like this so-called bathroom."

"Killjoy."

"Yeah." He dipped his head for one final, delectable taste of her. "I'll make it up to you."

"Is that a promise?"

"You can count on it. Now, let's get out of here."

Giving her bottom one final squeeze, he shifted around and carefully opened the door. Crouching low, he stepped out. "Remember, keep below the windows."

They took up residency on the floor, side by side, their backs against the bottom bunk bed.

"How long do we ride?" Jenny asked.

"Hopefully only until our hosts make their first stop."

"Hopefully?"

"It depends on where they stop. A gas station or rest area where they both get out of the truck should be fairly easy. If their next stop is home or a campsite for the night, it could make getting out of here without being seen, a little trickier."

TEN

For a while they rode in silence.

Jenny had crawled up on the bottom bunk to lie down, and Kyle stretched out, resting his head on the edge of the mattress. He closed his eyes, but sleep eluded him. Her teasing him about the school bus had taken him back. Made him think.

Over the last few days he'd remembered all the pain they'd caused each other, but he'd forgotten about the joy. The laughter. The things they'd shared. The places they'd made love.

Like the school bus.

During her summer break, she'd been working as a volunteer counselor at a camp for underprivileged children. One night she'd snuck out after midnight and met him in the parking lot. One thing had led to another, until they ended up in that bus. It had been hot and sweaty, and they'd been so eager for each other that nothing else mattered.

And there had been other times equally as unexpected: a midnight swim in the lake because the pool had been too tame, the night she'd talked him into her bedroom while the rest of the household slept, a picnic table in a deserted park during a summer rain shower, and the boathouse on her father's summer estate—especially the boathouse.

Jenny had been beautiful, sexy and adventurous. While he'd been the conservative one, afraid for her, not wanting to hurt her by letting anyone find out about their affair.

"What are you thinking about?"

Surprised, Kyle turned toward the bed. "I thought you were sleeping."

"Just drifting. You?"

He rested his back against the bunk. "I was thinking about the past . . ." *How from the very beginning I'd been unable to resist you.* ". . . about how things used to be between us."

For a moment she remained silent, then she said, "I think I fell in love with you the first time I saw you."

Kyle smiled. "Me too." Though they'd danced around each other for months, exchanging nothing more than sly glances and fleeting smiles.

"It sure took you long enough to do something about it."

Kyle laughed softly. "It wasn't appropriate. I was a federal marshal, assigned to protect your father." But in the end, that hadn't mattered. Maybe it had been inevitable that they had ended up in bed together. Just as they'd been destined to part.

"Jenny . . ." He hesitated, wanting suddenly to understand more about what happened between them. And why. "Tell me why you decided to become a teacher."

"Why now, Kyle?"

He shifted around to look at her. "Why not?"

"I don't know." She shrugged. "It just doesn't seem important."

"I think it is." Five years ago he'd thought he had all the answers—knew everything there was to know about Jennifer Brooks. But over the last few days he'd come to realize how wrong he'd been. Oh, he'd known her physically all right. But there was so much more to her. So much he'd never taken the time to learn about. "I want to know."

"It's not a very exciting story."

He brushed a stray strand of dark hair from her cheek. "Tell me anyway. We have time."

She seemed reluctant, but raised up on one elbow, reached over and claimed his hand, lacing her fingers through his. "It's because of a teacher I had my first year of boarding school. Her name was Mrs. Deets."

"You were fond of her?"

"Yes, but it was more than that. You see, I was only ten when I first went away to school."

"That's pretty young. Isn't it?"

"Maybe. But in my case, it was necessary. Though *I* didn't think so at the time. Evidently, I'd gotten out of hand. With my mother dead and Father involved with his career, I had a string of governesses. All of whom quit almost as quickly as Father hired them. I guess I was a bit spoiled."

Kyle grinned, perfectly able to see the child she'd been: beautiful, smart, pampered, and more than Crawford Brooks could ever handle.

She laughed, obviously reading his thoughts. "Okay, so I was a lot spoiled. But the point is, Father couldn't deal with a problem preadolescent daughter along with everything else. So, off to school I went." She paused, tucking her hair behind her ears.

"Of course, I threw a few major temper tantrums—which had never failed me before. But for the first time, Father stuck to his guns. He finally convinced me to go, somewhat willingly, by promising to take me to Colorado for the Christmas holidays."

She closed her eyes and smiled. "I was so excited. It was going to be the first time we ever went off on a vacation alone For once, I'd have him all to myself. That promise got me through those first few months living away from home."

Kyle leaned forward, resting both arms on the bed. He had a feeling he knew what was coming, and silently cursed Crawford Brooks.

When she continued, he heard the sadness in her voice. "I was all packed, waiting for him to pick me up. Our housekeeper showed up instead." Again she paused, and he could almost touch her disappointment—softened by years but still there. "Father had gotten tied up on a case and had to cancel our trip.

"While the other girls were leaving with parents, I was leaving with a housekeeper and chauffeur."

Kyle tightened his grip on her hand. "Enter Mrs. Deets?"

"Yeah." She threw him a smile, and he brought their joined hands to his lips and kissed her fingers. "I did what any spoiled, disappointed ten-year-old would do. I locked myself in my room and refused to open it for anyone but my father."

She laughed, and Kyle smiled, though he knew she'd forced the laughter. He could see how hard it had been on her. "Everyone was frantic, and I was convinced they'd have to get my father there before I'd open up." This time, her laugh was real. "So much for a ten-year-old's logic.

"Anyway, I don't know how, but Mrs. Deets talked me out of the room and ended up taking me home with *her*."

"The school allowed that?"

"Not usually. And to this day I don't know how she arranged it. But it was wonderful. Her husband and two daughters made me feel a part of everything. It was my first taste of a real family. Of a normal home life.

"After that, I spent some part of every holiday and summer with the Deetses. They became the family I never had, and they showed me what I wanted in my life. A family. And teaching naturally followed."

For several minutes neither of them spoke, and Kyle realized they'd broached the subject neither of them wanted to explore. For the past few days they'd occasionally touched on it, but basically had pushed it aside, not wanting to relive the pain they'd caused each other. After all, their time together now was temporary, no more than a few moments out of their lives.

Lives that would soon go in separate directions.

"I'm sorry, Jenny." He wished he had more than words to offer her. "I'm sorry I couldn't give you those things."

She looked up at him, a single tear slipped from her eye. "Me too, Kyle."

"Ah, Jenny. . . ." He reached over to brush away the tear, his hand lingering against her cheek.

For a moment, neither spoke. Then Jenny said, "Forget it. It's ancient history." She pulled back out of his reach and stretched out on the bed.

Two days ago he would have let it go. But then, two days ago he'd thought he understood what his relationship to Jenny was all about. He'd wanted to protect her. Now he realized the cost of protecting her had been his heart.

"Jenny, it's time we talked about this."

She closed her eyes. "I don't think so."

"Why?" He reached over and reclaimed her hand. "Because it's hard?"

"No, because we've been over it before. Countless times. And nothing has changed."

"How can you say that? Everything has changed."

"Like what, Kyle?" She rolled back over on her side, her wonderful brown eyes laced with sorrow. "Have I changed? I still want a family. And I'm doing what I love. Teaching. I can't give that up. And what about you? I've seen what you do for people. I know what you did for Samson. Are you ready to give all that up to work a nine-to-five job?"

"Jenny—" he started, though he didn't really have an answer for her. Not yet. All he knew was that he couldn't let her go. Not again. Not and survive it.

"Don't say anything, Kyle." Her voice cut him off, though it had softened. "We both know the truth. You can't change what you do. What you *are*. And I realize now, that I don't want you to change."

"So that's it?" he asked. "That's your answer. Once we get through this, we just go our separate ways?"

"There's no other way."

Kyle didn't agree. Everything had changed. He'd changed. He'd begun to realize that nothing mattered to him as much as this woman. She'd changed. Five years ago, she'd never have understood about the people he helped. But he held his thoughts close for the moment. First, he needed to get them through this. They needed to put Vittorio Casale and his threats behind them. Then he and

Jenny were going to have it out. Only this time, there was no way he'd let her walk away.

For the next couple of hours, as the highway spun out beneath them, Jenny went over their conversation in her head. Again and again, she poked and examined every word, every smile, every touch. If there had been another way for the conversation to have ended, a different path their words could have taken, she couldn't find it.

She and Kyle belonged in separate worlds.

Yet, she had meant every word she'd said. Though it had nearly killed her to say them. Especially when she'd looked into the warm depths of his blue-green eyes and seen him wavering. The woman she'd been seventy-two hours ago would have used that to bind him to her, to hold him close for the rest of their lives. Now, she couldn't do it.

He didn't belong to her. He belonged to all the people he could help and to the work he loved. Yet, there was a comfort she'd never felt before, a peace in knowing that it didn't change how he felt about her.

Kyle loved her.

Getting out of the trailer without being seen proved easier than Jenny could have hoped for. It was nearly dark and about four hours after leaving the diner. They pulled into a rest area, and both occupants of the truck headed for the rest rooms.

Kyle evidently saw their chance.

He ushered her outside and away from the trailer. And within minutes of dozing on a stranger's bed, she gratefully sank onto a wooden bench that was one of a group of picnic tables at the far end of the rest area. The day had begun to take its toll, and just the idea of confronting a pair of indignant trailer owners was more than she could handle at the moment.

Unfortunately, a place to stay the night seemed hours away. They still had no transportation and were obviously miles from anywhere.

"Wait here," Kyle said. "I'm going to see if I can get us a legitimate ride this time."

Jenny nodded, too tired to ask questions, and watched Kyle cross the lot and approach a couple of truck drivers. Briefly, she wished she could hear what they were saying. Kyle pointed toward her once, and she thought she saw money exchanged. Then she decided it didn't matter what Kyle said to get them a ride. They needed to keep moving. That was the important thing. And if there was a way, Kyle would find it.

A few minutes later, Kyle helped her into the cab of a mammoth truck.

More traveling. This time she kept silent, eventually drifting in and out of sleep, while Kyle and the truck driver chatted about inconsequential things: sports, weather, even an occasional comment about the country western songs that came from the truck's radio. Jenny settled closer beneath Kyle's protective arm, letting their conversation flow around her.

Hours later, they climbed down out of the cab, and Kyle lifted a hand in thanks to the driver.

As the truck moved off, Jenny turned toward the small roadside motel the driver had recommended. "I'm exhausted."

"I know you're tired, Jen, but we're not staying here." Kyle slipped his arm around her shoulders. "It's not safe."

"But—"

"We don't know who that truck driver will see or talk to before morning, and we can't take the chance it will be the wrong person. I saw a place about a half mile back. It'll be safer if we stay there."

They retraced the way they'd come along the highway. A half mile or twenty—Jenny couldn't say. She could no longer gauge time or distance. Any moment now, she thought she might fall down on the ground and go to sleep. But she managed to keep moving, drawing strength from Kyle's arm.

Finally they came to the place he'd mentioned: a small run-down motel consisting of a dozen or so separate cabins. Another time perhaps and she would have balked at staying at a place that looked more fit for cockroaches than humans. Tonight, she was just too tired to care.

Kyle checked them in, and she couldn't remember ever being more grateful for the simple pleasure of shedding her clothes, donning one of Kyle's shirts, and sinking into cool, clean sheets.

She was asleep before her head hit the pillow.

The storm woke her.

Wind and rain lashed at the night, and for one terrifying second Jenny couldn't remember where she was. Then a deafening crash of thunder sent tremors through the shabby wooden cottage, while a flash of lightning followed so close that the two seemed inseparable.

Kyle?

She reached for him and found cold, empty space. Sitting bolt upright, she scanned the room, frightened that he'd left her already. Then she saw him sitting near the windows, the drapes open, his hand wrapped around the gun in his lap.

"Kyle?"

He turned at the sound of her voice. Through the rain-smeared window, a lone streetlight cast eerie shifting shadows across his face. "Go back to sleep, Jenny."

"What about you?" She pushed aside the covers and moved to the edge of the bed. "Why are you just sitting there?"

"I'm watching." He turned to the window. "If I were Casale, I'd make my move at night."

She slipped from bed and went to him, first

closing the drapes against the storm, and then sinking to her knees in front of him.

"Casale," she said, taking the gun from Kyle's hand and setting it on the nearby table, "doesn't know we're here." Edging his legs apart, she slid between them and leaned forward to press her lips against his bare chest. He tasted of soap and man, stirring a sharp feminine heat deep within her.

He moved his hands to her head, submerging his fingers in her hair. She sighed and turned to rest her cheek against him, while his dark masculine smell filled her senses. Idly, he stroked her scalp, sending shivers of pleasure through her. She could have stayed like that forever but sensed that for once this wasn't about her.

Now, tonight, Kyle *needed* her.

Lifting her head, she looked up at him. He'd closed his eyes and rested his head against the chair back, and she could feel the exhaustion—and something else, something much heavier—weighing on him.

"What is it, Kyle? What's wrong?"

For several long moments he didn't answer, while outside the wind and rain continued their battle. Clashing thunder, another flash of light, and finally he said, "They're getting close, Jen. Real close. And *we're* running out of options."

She closed her eyes briefly and let her chin rest against his chest. "You'll find a way," she said, believing it. "I know it."

"We should have run. I should have taken you

away instead of bringing you back to Washington. We could have disappeared."

"Hush." Jenny pressed her fingers to his lips. "You did the right thing. *We* did the right thing."

He opened his eyes finally and lifted his head to look down at her. "How can you be sure?"

"It's like you said. If we'd run, Casale would have won. And the next person who came up against him may have folded. We're doing the right thing, Kyle."

A long silence followed. Outside, the wind continued to whip the rain against the windows in fits and starts. While inside, Jenny sensed Kyle raged against a different type of storm.

"What if I can't protect you?" he said finally, in a voice so soft, she almost didn't hear him.

She shook her head and reached up to caress his cheek. "It doesn't matter."

"Jenny—"

"Enough." Again, she pressed her fingers to his lips. Then, before he could say anything else, she kissed his chest letting her lips linger this time against his skin. She heard his sharp intake of breath as she found one taut male nipple. She teased it first with her mouth, sucking and licking, and then gently grazed it with her teeth.

He groaned and gripped her arms, as if to pull her up.

"No," she said, pulling away and sliding her hands to unfasten the snap of his jeans. "Not yet."

She took her time loving him, first brushing her

face against the soft hair spiraling downward beneath the denim of his jeans, and then running her tongue over the hard ridges of his stomach. She could feel his erection, hard and ready beneath her, and the answering dampness between her own thighs.

But she wasn't done with him yet. Not nearly.

He'd seen so much evil, his days and nights waltzing with death. Tonight, she'd give him a taste of life.

Drawing away, she moved her hands to his legs, working the muscles, one leg and then the other, from knees to groin, always stopping just short of touching the hard bulge beneath his jeans.

"Ah, Jenny . . ."

"Do you like that?" she whispered, her voice breathy as she tried to control her own needs while answering his.

"Oh, God, yes."

"Good. Because I'm just getting started." She pressed her face against his arousal, feeling the hard throb of his desire through the heavy fabric. "Before I get done with you, you'll be begging for mercy."

"I'm already begging."

Laughing softly, Jenny shifted back on her heels. She used her hands again, this time rubbing his sex through the denim until he groaned, his hands gripping the arms of the chair.

When she thought he could take no more, she moved to his zipper, easing it down over his arousal.

Then, while he lifted up, she gripped the waistband of his jeans and pulled them down and off his legs.

She moved her hands back to his thighs, feeling them quiver beneath her hands. Slowly, she inched upward, teasing and taunting him, until finally she wrapped her hands around him. Her eyes closed, she stroked him, the muscles at her core contracting with each motion. Wanting. Needing. Waiting for the feel of him inside her.

Suddenly, he grabbed her wrists, pulling her up to stretch across him, his mouth taking hers. It took her breath away—the demanding pressure of his mouth and the need spiraling within her.

Then, she felt his hands, finding their way beneath the thin cotton shirt to the sensitive skin beneath. He stroked her backside. Once. Twice. And then grabbed her thighs, pulling them up and forward until she straddled him, and he thrust into her.

Jenny cried out. Losing herself. "I love you, Kyle."

ELEVEN

When Kyle came back to his senses, the storm had passed, leaving only the rain, steadily beating against the wooden roof.

Gathering Jenny in his arms, he carried her to the bed. She mumbled something incoherent, but he simply kissed the top of her silky head and lay her down on the rumpled sheets. Then he crawled in beside her and pulled her close.

She had opened his eyes.

Earlier, sitting in the dark with the demons of the last three days nipping at his soul, he'd decided to take her and run. As soon as the sun touched the horizon, they'd be on their way. Anywhere but east. He'd come too close to losing her to continue down that path, and he'd about used up all his tricks.

Then she'd come to him. Like a storm-borne witch, she'd shattered his demons and chased all thoughts of fleeing with the touch of her lips and the sound of her voice.

He'd never known she could be so giving, not just of her body, but of herself. It made him see her in an entirely different light. As much as he loved her, he'd always thought of her as spoiled—pampered and sheltered—by her father and by her station in life.

It had been an illusion she'd shattered tonight.

She'd made him see what he'd already known, but forgotten in his fear for her. They were going up against Casale for all the others who might someday face the man. They were making a stand. He and Jenny. It may be his job, but Jenny was willing to put her life on the line right next to him.

Kyle woke first, with Jenny still tucked against him, her bare backside nestled snugly against his lower belly. His body responded instantly, hardening and thickening, eager to take what the feel of her promised.

Yet, for several minutes he just held her, the rhythm of her steady breathing like a balm to his fevered senses. Last night had been wild and tumultuous, but today, with the early-morning sun sneaking past the edges of the heavy curtains, he felt content. Waking with her in his arms again was as sweet as the new day, and he planned to cherish every moment.

Who knew if he'd ever experience either again?

Then Jenny murmured something in her sleep, and holding her was no longer enough.

Slipping a hand from beneath the covers, he smoothed the hair away from her face and neck, seeking the tender skin beneath. He kissed her lightly, brushing his lips along her nape, while returning his hand to the warmth beneath the blanket and the gentle swell of one breast.

She sighed softly as her nipple hardened beneath his fingers.

Kyle smiled, remembering all the other times he'd awakened with her; mornings like this one in so many ways. Yet, different too. None had ever been sweeter. Or more melancholy. He knew from the past that he could bring her along, almost to the point of climax, before she awoke, hot and eager.

He continued stroking softly, letting his hands drift from one breast to the other, circling each nipple until it puckered into a stiff point.

This time she moaned and shifted her bottom against him, pulling a matching groan from him as his body grew harder still. He abandoned her breasts, moving his hand down over the soft skin of her belly to the sweet vee between her thighs. He found her damp and ready, and as he dipped his fingers into her moist hollow, she opened for him.

He went slowly, sliding his fingers up and back, teasing the sensitive nub, then slipping away to explore deeper, only to return again to the core of her desire. By the time she climaxed, trembling and convulsing against his hand, she'd awakened fully.

Turning her over, he sought her lips and positioned himself between her thighs. She whimpered again as he sank into her, her arms banding around his hips, hands open, pressing against his buttocks as she arched up to meet his thrust.

He stilled for a moment, releasing her mouth and lifting his head just enough to look into her eyes—hot, honey-brown eyes, that returned his gaze with a mixture of sleep and desire.

"Good morning," he whispered.

She smiled and nipped at his mouth. "Yes. It is."

He laughed and felt her shift beneath him, teasing him as he had her. Then his control slipped, and he lost himself in her.

An hour later, Kyle reluctantly climbed from bed.

He'd lingered too long already, enjoying the woman beside him, when he knew they needed to move on. But he didn't regret spending the morning making love to her. They'd been through so much, and the worst could still be ahead of them. He'd wanted to give Jenny one last taste of hope before venturing beyond the relative safety of these four walls. And now he couldn't resist bending down to claim one more kiss, before leaving her.

Because, one way or the other, it ended today.

With that in mind, he took time to prepare, showering and dressing carefully while going over their options in his head.

First, he ruled out public transportation. Casale's men would have every bus and train station between here and DC covered. In the same vein, hitching another ride would be risky. Casale had eyes and ears everywhere. No doubt the word was on the street to watch for a couple looking for a ride into Washington. They might get lucky and find a driver with no connection to the crime lord. Then again, they could walk right into a trap.

That didn't leave much, but Casale hadn't won yet.

Abandoning his biker persona, Kyle dressed in the flannel shirt and jeans he'd worn in Georgia. Chances were Casale wouldn't be fooled by a simple change of clothing, but Kyle planned to use every possible trick at his disposal. Even if it only gained him a minute or two before they recognized him, it might mean the difference between life and death.

When he came out of the bathroom, Jenny was sitting on the edge of the bed, watching a news report from a local station.

"That's the latest from New York," said a woman with a microphone. "This is Debra St. John, live from Central Park. Back to you, Mike."

"Jenny—"

She held up a hand to cut him off "Wait."

The picture switched to a well-dressed man at a news desk. "Thank you, Debra. Now we take you live to Washington for an update on the disappearance of Jennifer Brooks. Daughter of Federal Appellate Judge Crawford Brooks."

The picture switched to the front of the federal courthouse, where a group of reporters surrounded Crawford Brooks as he emerged from the building. Questions sprang at him from all directions.

Then Brooks lifted a hand and the group quieted.

"I'm afraid there's nothing new to report," Brooks said. "There still has been no word from or about my daughter." As always, he sounded smooth and confident. Only those who knew him well would notice the slight tremor in his hands and the fear in his eyes. "I have every faith in the Justice Department and the officers directly involved. They *will* find Jennifer. Unharmed."

"Judge Brooks, what about the Casale case?" one reporter asked, shoving his microphone in front of the judge.

"Philip Casale's appeal starts tomorrow."

"Are you going to continue with the case?"

"I have been appointed to the case. Yes. There's no reason for me not to continue."

"But what about the allegations that Vittorio Casale is responsible for the disappearance of your daughter?"

"There is no evidence at this time to link either Vittorio or Philip Casale to the disappearance of my daughter. Until there is, I have no comment."

"But Your Honor—"

"That's all for now." Brooks raised a hand and

turned. The marshals who'd been standing nearby closed ranks behind him. Kyle winced when he recognized DeMitri as one of the men flanking the judge.

The picture switched to a female reporter standing in front of a row of cherry trees, their bright pink blossoms rustling in a spring breeze. "Well there you have it, Mike. It's been three days since Jennifer Brooks disappeared from what we've just recently learned was a federal safe house in Georgia. The authorities—"

Kyle moved to the television and shut it off. Then he sat next to Jenny and took her hand. "I'm sorry, Jenny."

"We're so close. Surely if we went to the police—"

"The police will turn us over to federal marshals, and then we'll be separated. I'll be called in for debriefing, and they'll assign someone else to you. They'll either take you to your father or into hiding again. Possibly both. But either way, you won't be safe for long." He squeezed her hand. "We're only about a hundred and fifty miles from Washington. I'll get you to there."

"But even then, I won't be safe from Casale."

"Once we plug the leak, we'll have the department resources to protect you. Until then, you have to trust me. We'll get on the road, then we'll try to get through to your father again."

She smiled tightly and nodded. "Okay." Then,

in an obvious attempt to lighten the mood, she said, "So, how are we traveling today?"

Kyle smiled, amazed again at her strength. "We need a car."

"Are you going to steal one?"

She said it so matter-of-factly, he almost laughed. Except it wasn't funny. He *would* steal a car if he thought it necessary to ensure her safety. Fortunately, he wasn't to that point yet. "No. We're going to buy one."

"You have that much cash with you?"

She'd learned quickly. Credit didn't exist when you were on the run. At least, not usually. But they were in the homestretch and about to make a dash for the finish line. "I have about six hundred dollars," he said. "We'll need another four or five to get transportation we can rely on."

"You're not going to steal money, are you?"

This time he did laugh. "Ever heard of an ATM machine?"

She shook her head. "You're nuts. I'm sure they can trace the transaction."

"No doubt. And if *I* were DeMitri, I'd be watching for it. But I figure we have thirty minutes before he sends someone after us. We'll just have to make sure we're long gone by then."

Finding a car proved easier than Kyle had hoped.

The first lot they tried had several fitting their

needs: cheap, nondescript, and with a large enough engine to deliver speed in case of an emergency. He selected the best of the bunch and gave the salesman a hundred dollars to hold it. Then he and Jenny went off to get the rest of the cash. Less than an hour later, they were on the road heading toward Washington once again.

Things had gone so smoothly, it made Kyle nervous.

On top of that, Jenny had been particularly quiet since the news report they'd heard about her disappearance. He knew she was concerned about her father and frightened about what lay ahead of them.

"Jenny, are you okay?" he asked.

"I'm fine."

He didn't buy it. "Anything you want to talk about?"

For a moment she didn't answer. Then she said, "I was thinking about our relationship before I moved to Atlanta." She paused, and he sensed her searching for the right words. "Why wouldn't you let me tell my father about us?"

The question surprised him, though it shouldn't have he supposed. It was just another of the problems between them when they'd gone their separate ways. Maybe it was time for the truth. "I didn't think he'd approve."

"I know that much." She shifted sideways on the seat to look at him. "Did you think it would matter to me?"

"It mattered to me." He glanced over at her, seeing the questions on her face.

"Jenny . . ." He hesitated, afraid she wouldn't understand. Hell, he didn't know if *he* understood anymore. Things had been so different five years ago. At least they had seemed different. "You were so much more than I'd ever dreamed of in a woman. You deserved more than I could give you."

"Are you talking about money?"

"Yes. No. It was more than that."

"What was it, Kyle?" An edge of anger had crept into her voice.

He hesitated again, uncomfortable explaining this to her. Still, he knew she had a right to know. "All those months I spent with you and your father, accompanying the two of you to social events"—his hands seemed to tighten of their own around the steering wheel—"it made me see our relationship for what it was. Or what I thought it was."

"I don't understand."

"I know you don't." He paused, taking a deep breath. "I was a hired hand, Jenny. One of the help."

"What are you talking about? You're a federal marshal."

"Pinning a government tag on it doesn't change the facts. I was a bodyguard in a tux."

A strained silence fell between them. Kyle could sense Jenny's discomfort with what he'd just told her. And possibly, she'd started to understand the real reason he hadn't left Washington with her.

"I never knew you felt that way," she said finally. "You never told me."

"No. I couldn't. I loved you." He threw her another quick glance before turning back to the road. "And I thought you were entitled to all the good things in life."

He sensed her pull away. When he looked over at her again, she'd turned to stare out the side window.

"Jenny," he said, "you deserved someone better."

"What right had you to make that decision for me?"

He hesitated, and then said, "You're forgetting that you were the one who left Washington. You were the one who went off in search of your dream."

"And I asked you to come with me. Begged you."

"You knew that I wouldn't."

She looked away, and he knew she'd finally seen the truth. When she looked at him again, a wash of tears filled her eyes. "And if I hadn't left? If I'd stayed in Washington? What would you have done then?"

He considered lying. It would be easier on both of them. He could still convince her that their parting was as much her fault as his. But somewhere along the way, sometime in the last few days he'd learned that Jenny didn't need him protecting her with lies. What she needed from him was the truth.

"If you'd stayed in Washington, I would have ended our relationship."

Jenny rested her head against the seat back, realizing she'd always known it. Before she'd left Washington for Atlanta, Kyle had planned to end their affair. Only she'd beat him to it. That's why she'd chosen that particular time to change her life, to step out of the harsh glare of her father's world.

They continued on in silence for the next half hour. Then, as they came up on the outskirts of a small town, Kyle pulled into a gas station and stopped the car near the pay phone.

"Okay," he said, turning to face her. "Let's see if we can get through to your father. But remember, they're going to try and keep you on the line. Don't let them. You have less than two minutes before the call is traced." He glanced at his watch. "I'll time it for you. All you have to worry about is getting your father on the line. Tell him you're safe. Nothing else. Then get off."

Jenny nodded, and they climbed out of the car.

As she dialed, Kyle stayed close, leaning against the glass edge of the phone booth, while keeping his eyes on the area around them.

Jenny held her breath as the phone rang three times.

Crawford Brooks answered on the fourth ring. "Hello."

For a moment, she couldn't speak. She hadn't expected to get through. "Dad?"

Kyle edged closer.

"Jennifer? Is that you?"

"Yes, yes." She was crying now and couldn't stop. "It's me."

"My, God, where are you? Are you all right?"

"I'm fine. I'm with Kyle." She'd forgotten all the guidelines he'd set down for her. After all, this was her father. "We're—"

"Munroe?" her father said. "Put him on. Quick!"

Surprised, she handed the phone to Kyle. "He wants to talk to you."

Kyle took the phone, and she stepped out of the way. "Sir," he said, his voice hesitant.

It was difficult listening to a one-sided conversation; especially when so much was at stake. She watched Kyle's face for some indication of what her father was saying, but couldn't tell a thing. Kyle's expression remained impassive, while his eyes continued to scan the area around them.

"Are you sure?" Kyle said, glancing at his watch.

Jenny saw they had about forty-five seconds left before reaching the two-minute mark. She wrapped her arms tightly around her waist, knowing that no matter what her father was telling Kyle, he'd hang up before allowing time for a trace.

"Yes, I know the place," Kyle said. His gaze met Jenny's, and she saw his uncertainty. "Yes, sir. Thirty minutes."

Kyle hung up the phone.

"So," she said, "what's going on?"

"Not here." He glanced around and nodded at a chain restaurant across the street. "Let's get some coffee."

As Kyle led her across the street, Jenny didn't know what to think or feel. She'd finally spoken to her father, and the joy of that struggled to surface. Five years without hearing his voice, and she hadn't realized until this trouble started how much she'd missed him. Yet, she was afraid to believe it was all over, and anxious to hear what he and Kyle had spoken about.

By the time they slid into the booth of the busy restaurant, she thought she'd burst. Still, Kyle took his time, ordering coffee, as if getting his own thoughts sorted out before speaking. Once the waitress left, however, Jenny couldn't wait any longer.

"Kyle," she said, "tell me what he said."

"On the surface, it's good news. According to your father, you were right about Philip Casale. He's the leak. He's been paying off several guards to look the other way while he used the prison's computers to hack into the Justice Department mainframe. It explains a lot."

"Like how they knew I was in Atlanta. But how did they know about the cabin in the mountains? There must be more than one safe house in the Atlanta area."

"Most likely by a process of elimination. They could have had a man waiting at each location on file with the Atlanta office. When we arrived at the cabin, they put out the word. Then it was a matter of a few hours to assemble their men at one place." Kyle hesitated, and she knew he wasn't quite convinced.

"Your father wants me to bring you in. He's arranged for a pickup. Several other marshals will meet us about thirty minutes from here."

"What's still bothering you?" she asked.

"How did they know about Samson's?"

"Isn't he in the files?"

"Yes. But how did they know I'd head there? There are at least a dozen other places we could have gone. Or I could have taken you someplace completely out of the system."

"Maybe they sent men out to all the locations to watch for us. Like they did the safe house."

"Possibly." Kyle paused before adding, "The best part is, DeMitri is evidently in the clear." Yet, he didn't sound completely convinced of that either.

Jenny closed her hands over his. "So what do we do now?"

He hesitated again, then seemed to make a decision. "I take you to your father. Come on," he said tossing some bills on the table. "Let's get going."

"Wait, I need to stop in the ladies' room."

Kyle glanced at the hallway to the rest rooms. He could easily watch it from here. "Okay. I'll wait here."

Jenny went off to the ladies' room, and Kyle

waited, going over and over in his head what Crawford Brooks had told him. Something was missing—some piece of information that would tie everything together, that would explain how Casale knew about Samson without DeMitri being involved.

Then Jenny stepped back into the dining room, and fear ripped through Kyle.

A man held her arm, keeping her close to his side. Kyle didn't have to see the gun wedged at her back to know it was there. Slipping the Beretta from its holster, he shoved it into his jacket pocket.

Jenny's life depended on how he handled the next few minutes, how he handled the fear. Controlling his own fear was easy; turning a deaf ear to Jenny's was another thing altogether. But he needed to do both or the game would be over before it even started.

Jenny's eyes locked on his, her dark brown eyes wide, frightened and begging him for help. Then Casale's man zeroed in on him, and recognition coiled in Kyle's gut. Avery Maxwell. A man of a different ilk from the big, clumsy men who'd followed Kyle and Jenny the day before. Hell, he wasn't even one of Casale's regulars, but a gun for hire. Rattling him wasn't going to be easy.

But Kyle had to try.

He thought of taking a shot as Maxwell and Jenny walked passed him, heading for the exit, but immediately dismissed the idea. The restaurant was crowded, and once bullets started flying, people died.

Instead, he slid from the booth and followed them outside.

Maxwell had already swung around, putting Jenny between himself and Kyle.

"Let her go," Kyle commanded, keeping his voice low. "And you can walk away."

"Get real, Munroe." Maxwell kept moving, edging sideways toward a white van parked alongside the building. "You try and take me, and she'll be dead before you get off a shot."

Kyle kept pace with them, his eyes on the other man. "There are federal agents all over this place," he bluffed. "You're not taking her out of here."

"Good try." Maxwell grinned. "But I happen to know you're alone. That's the way you like to work, isn't it, Munroe? Alone."

Kyle bit back his frustration and pulled his gun from his jacket. Taking aim at the other man's head, Kyle said, "This is your last chance. Let the lady go."

They'd reached the van, and the side panel slid open.

"Not on your life." With his arm around her waist, Maxwell fell backward into the van, pulling Jenny with him.

A second man stepped around them, and the last thing Kyle saw was a shotgun barrel and two flashes of light.

TWELVE

Jenny screamed as the bullets slammed into Kyle's chest, dropping him to the ground.

"He's down!" yelled the shooter, ramming the panel door closed. "Get us out of here!"

The van shot forward, and her captor clamped a hand across Jenny's mouth. She fought him, throwing herself against the arm around her waist and dragging at the wrist near her mouth, breaking his hold enough to sink her teeth into his palm.

Growling in pain, he yanked his hand away.

Again she screamed, struggling to get free.

Kyle. She needed to get to him.

Her struggles only seemed to make the man holding her angrier. He tightened his grip on her waist and grabbed one of her arms, twisting it behind her. "Shut up, bitch. Or I'll break your arm."

The pain swept her breath away, and Jenny sank

against him, realizing as the van sped forward she'd lost all hope of escape. Kyle was beyond her reach.

"That's better," said Casale's man.

She fought the sob that threatened to escape. She wouldn't cry, wouldn't give these men the satisfaction. Instead, she mustered the last of her breath. "Go to hell."

The man laughed, and the hopelessness of her situation overwhelmed her. Like a rag doll, he tossed her against the side of the van. "Sit down."

Jenny sank to the floor.

Then he proceeded to bind her arms and legs, blindfold and gag her. She didn't fight him. It didn't matter anymore what they did to her. All she could see was Kyle lying alone in that parking lot. Dead.

The pain was much worse than Kyle had expected.

He'd known that a shotgun blast would knock you unconscious. Vest or no vest, a man couldn't stand against the brute force of such a weapon. He'd expected to feel like he'd been struck in the chest with a hammer. And he did. He hadn't expected the searing pain that made him want to check and make sure the bullets hadn't blown their way through the soft body armor he'd worn under his shirt.

He shifted, and a second source of pain shot through his head. He must have hit it going down.

"Hey, mister, you all right?"

Kyle opened his eyes slowly. A waiter from the restaurant hovered over him.

"No," Kyle said, "I'm *not* all right. I feel like I was hit with a round of double-ought shot."

The other man grinned. "Good thing you was wearing that vest."

Kyle lifted his pounding head just enough to see that his shirt had been ripped open to reveal the vest underneath. "Yeah, good thing."

He made a move to get up, and the stranger took his arm. "Here, let me help you."

As he struggled to his feet, Kyle noticed the small group of people who'd gathered around them.

"You a cop or something?" the waiter asked.

"Or something." Kyle scanned the highway. "How long have I been out?"

"Five, six minutes."

Kyle mentally groaned. Too long. Casale's men would be miles from here by now. "The men who shot me. In the white van. Which way did they go?"

The man shrugged.

Kyle reluctantly pulled out his wallet and showed his badge. "I'm from the U.S. Marshals Service. You've just witnessed the kidnapping of a protected witness and the attempted murder of a federal officer. Now, which way did the van go?"

Just then, several sedans, lights flashing and sirens blaring, turned into the restaurant parking lot, parting the small crowd of onlookers.

Kyle glanced at the waiter, who shrugged again. "I called the police as soon as I heard the shots."

"Great." Kyle put a hand over the searing pain in his chest. He needed to go after Jenny, and now he'd be tied up explaining himself to his superiors.

DeMitri jumped from the first car and came toward him. "Are you all right?"

Kyle went cold inside. "What the hell are *you* doing here?"

"We were on our way to meet you and Miss Brooks when we heard the call go out over the police band. We figured it was you and thought you could use some help."

"*Your* kind of help I don't need."

DeMitri frowned and took a step back. "You think I had something to do with this?"

"It all adds up."

DeMitri shook his head. "It was Philip Casale. He hacked his way into our files."

"That's what Crawford Brooks thinks."

"Look, we found large, recent deposits in certain prison officials' bank accounts. And our computer systems people discovered traces of the break-ins. We can even identify which files were looked at. A little more time and they'll be able to trace it back to the phone line used."

"How do I know he was working alone? How do I know *you* weren't helping him?"

DeMitri's face clouded. "Look, Munroe, I don't have to take this from you. If you think you've got some kind of proof that I'm dirty, fine. File a complaint." He turned and started to walk away.

"They followed me from Samson's," Kyle said,

effectively stopping the other man in his tracks. "You're the only one who knew that's where we'd gone."

DeMitri spun back around and in two quick strides closed the distance between them again. "Look, Munroe, when this is all over I *might* just accept your apology." He jabbed a finger at Kyle's chest. "But right now, you're pissing me off. I don't know how they found you at Samson's. Are you so damn sure *you* didn't make a mistake? Because from where I sit, you've got yourself so tied up over that woman, you can't think straight.

"But I'll give you a clue: *If* I were working for Casale, you and Miss Brooks would never have made it out of Georgia. I'd have turned you over to him the minute you two climbed down into that tunnel."

Kyle stepped back.

"That's right," DeMitri continued. "I'm the one who scouted that house in Georgia. And I knew exactly where that tunnel led. *If* I was on Casale's payroll, his men would have been waiting for you when you crawled out of that hole."

Kyle felt like an idiot.

Everything DeMitri had said was true. Even about Jenny. Since the moment Kyle had seen her again, he hadn't been thinking straight. He'd made the mistakes. And now Casale's men had taken her. If he'd trusted DeMitri . . .

"Come on, Munroe." DeMitri laid a hand on Kyle's shoulder, pulling him from his thoughts.

"Think about it. You've known me for years. Do you really think I would sell out to a man like Casale?"

Kyle took a deep breath and closed his eyes briefly. He'd greatly misjudged a man he'd called his friend. "You're right. I'm sorry."

"Well . . ." DeMitri pressed his lips together and nodded. "It ain't over yet, so there's no time for that. So what do we do now, hotshot?"

Kyle met the other man's gaze and smiled his thanks. "Now, we go after Jenny."

She couldn't have said how long she lay on the floor of the van: hours or days. Nor did she care. Not with Kyle gone.

It all seemed so foolish now; her claims of needing the kind of life Kyle couldn't give her. When in fact she could have had everything with Kyle: a home and family, her career, and the only man she'd ever loved. *If* she'd been willing to risk it. *If* she'd been willing to live with his job.

Oh, she knew what he'd said earlier about his breaking off their relationship if she hadn't. But the thing was, saying it didn't make it true. Who knew what a little more time would have done for them? He might have eventually come to see that the last thing she considered him was hired help.

Funny, now that she had nothing, she realized that the only thing that had mattered, the only thing she really needed in that long list was Kyle himself.

With that thought her apathy turned to anger. Then to hate.

Kyle had died trying to protect her. And so she *had* to survive. She would make sure the man who'd shot Kyle paid for his crime. But more than that, she wanted to see—she *would* see—the man who'd ordered the shooting, Vittorio Casale, put away for life.

Finally the van slowed and turned, and the road grew bumpy, jarring her against the bare metal floor until she felt each bump and hole. Again the pain didn't matter. She concentrated on her anger, on seeing Casale pay for Kyle's death.

Abruptly, the van came to a stop.

Someone untied her feet and dragged her out of the van. She knew immediately they were outside the city. She could smell the freshly mown grass and the clean, clear air. It seemed odd to recognize such wonderfully normal scents under such abnormal circumstances.

Still gagged, blindfolded, and her hands bound, she was led inside a building. A house, she guessed, first from the smell of household cleansers and furniture polish, then from the feel of thick carpet beneath her feet. She tried to pay attention to the directions they took, but it was pointless. They walked too far with too many turns. She actually thought they might be leading her in circles to disorient her.

It was working.

When they finally stopped, and her blindfold and gag were removed, she recognized the man who had dragged her into the van.

"If you promise to behave," he said, "I'll release your hands. Otherwise, you can spend the rest of your life tied up."

Jenny shot him what she hoped was a murderous look, but held her tongue. Maybe if she appeared to cooperate, they'd let down their guard. Besides, she didn't want them thinking of her as a threat.

The man chuckled, as if reading her thoughts. But he removed the last of her bonds and left, leaving her standing in the middle of a large, ornate bedroom. Despite silk wallpaper and drapes, deep plush carpet and antique furnishings, the room was still a prison. No matter how expensively appointed.

She crossed to the windows and drew back the heavy drapes, only to find bars. Next she tried the bathroom, with its marble floors, brass fittings, and whirlpool tub. However, there was only one way in and out of that room as well. Returning to the bedroom, she tried the last door. It turned out to be a closet.

Frustrated, she came back to the center of the room.

For a moment, she stared at the large fourposter bed, and was tempted to curl up and weep. But then she turned away and took up a position in a chair facing the door.

They wouldn't make her cry.

There was more to her than they knew, more than they could see. She was Jennifer Brooks, daughter to one of Washington's most influential men. And she'd spent the last four days with a federal marshal who had taught her a thing or two. Not only wouldn't they break her, she intended to make them pay.

Kyle stood at the edge of the woods, outside an estate rumored to belong to Vittorio Casale. It had taken him several hours to locate the place, to get the information he needed to find Jenny. Now he was ready, waiting for the last minutes of daylight to fade from the western sky.

Casale had surrounded himself with two heavily guarded acres, including a ten-foot stone wall, surveillance cameras, and roaming guards. The fence and the guards Kyle could handle. It was the cameras that worried him. He'd spent an hour in a nearby tree trying to locate them and came up with five between here and the back of the mansion. If he'd spotted them all, he might be able to make it to the house unseen. If not, this was going to be a real short trip.

"You're out of your mind," DeMitri said beside him. "This is just the kind of crazy thinking I was talking about earlier."

Kyle made one final check of his Beretta and

secured it in its holster. "You have a better suggestion?"

"We don't even know for sure she's in there."

"She's in there." He pulled a dark ski mask down over his head.

"Then wait for the search warrant."

"Five minutes after we hit those front gates with a search warrant, Jenny will be gone." *Or dead.* Though he couldn't voice that thought aloud. "*If we can even get a search warrant, considering we have nothing but suspicion to link Casale to Jenny's disappearance.*"

DeMitri grabbed his arm. "What good are you going to do her if you get yourself killed?"

"I have no intentions of dying. Now, are you going to give me a boost up that wall, or are you going to stand there and argue with me all night?"

DeMitri cursed. "Okay, you've got one hour to get in and out. After that, I'm bringing in the troops. Search warrant or not."

Kyle grinned. In an hour he'd either be back here with Jenny, or he'd be dead. "You've got a deal."

A few minutes later, he lay atop the wall, scanning the grounds between the perimeter and the back of the mansion. When he was sure it was clear, he dropped inside. Again, he held his position for a moment, before slowly starting toward the house. He kept down, close to what little cover existed, while avoiding the cameras.

Finally he came to the last rise in back of the mansion.

Lying flat on the ground, he watched the house. He spotted two men sitting near the back door, talking and smoking. He didn't see any weapons, but that didn't mean anything. A man like Casale surrounded himself with hired guns. Kyle had no doubt these two fit that category.

And as long as they stayed put, Kyle couldn't move.

There was only one way into the mansion: a door his sources claimed wasn't wired into the central alarm system. The idea of Casale making such an obvious mistake, made Kyle nervous. But at the moment, he was out of options. He needed to get into that house, and that unalarmed door was the only possibility.

Except those men stood right in his path.

Finally one of them pulled a walkie-talkie from his back pocket. Kyle frowned, wondering what was happening. Then, as the men took off toward the front, he decided he didn't care. Seeing his chance, he headed in the opposite direction, toward the far side of the house.

He'd been told there was an extension on the west wing of the mansion, a piece of the original two-hundred-year-old structure that had once stood on these grounds. At one corner of the older section he found what he was looking for. A door leading down into a root cellar.

Breaking the lock was a snap, and he made his

way down the concrete steps, lowering the door above him. The darkness closed in, but he took deep breaths and switched on the flashlight he'd hooked to his belt. He'd gotten through the tunnel for Jenny, he could get through this as well.

With the door leading into the cellar, he didn't bother with the lock. He broke the glass and slipped his hand inside and opened it. Pushing through the door, he stepped into a large room and instantly felt the confines of the dark little stairway recede.

Drawing his Beretta, he crossed the room. He saw the laser sensor two seconds before he tripped it.

"Damn!" Breaking into a run, he started down the hallway.

He should have been watching for laser or motion sensors; he knew better than to think Casale would have left one of his doors unalarmed. Now Casale had been alerted to the presence of an intruder before Kyle was ready.

He came around a corner and nearly collided with four of Casale's hired guns.

Still sitting in the chair, Jenny had just dozed off when the door opened and one of Casale's goons stepped into the room.

"Come on," he snapped, though he looked uncomfortable giving orders. "Mr. Casale wants to see you."

Jenny considered refusing, but quickly dismissed the idea. It would serve no purpose to try to thwart Casale at this point. If he wanted to see her, his hired thug would make sure she got there. With or without her cooperation. And it would be a lot more comfortable arriving on her own two feet.

Crossing the room, she stepped through the door and leveled a haughty stare at him. "Okay, Igor, let's go see your boss."

"My name's not Igor."

"Really, could have fooled me." He started to take her arm, but she pulled away. "That's not necessary. Just tell me which way to go, and I'll walk myself."

He hesitated, obviously unsure what to do, and then drew a gun from the holster under his jacket. "Okay. Just remember I'm right behind you."

"How could I forget?"

As they made their way through a labyrinth of corridors, Jenny tried to memorize their route. It was the first time she'd been outside the locked room since they'd brought her there, and the place was enormous. Even as used to wealth as she was, the opulence struck her. Overstated, new money, she thought. Miles of it.

Finally they stopped in front of massive oak doors.

Her escort stepped up beside her and this time succeeded in grabbing her arm. "Don't give me any reason to hurt you."

He pushed through the doors, and Jenny came face-to-face with Vittorio Casale.

She would have recognized him anywhere, though she'd never even seen a picture of him. Years ago, traveling in her father's circles, she'd learned to recognize the men with power. They possessed a certain unmistakable aura, and Vittorio Casale reeked of it.

"Ah, Miss Brooks," he said. "Welcome. How good of you to join us."

The brute holding her arm pulled her farther into the room.

That's when she spotted the man tied to a chair.

"Kyle!" She yanked her arm free and rushed to his side, sinking to the floor next to him and touching his face to make sure he was real.

"You okay?" he asked, his voice soft, his eyes searching hers.

"Yes. But I thought—"

The man who'd brought her from the room grabbed her arm and pulled her away.

Kyle's gaze shifted to the crime lord. "You're just getting yourself in deeper, Casale. You touch her, and Crawford Brooks will nail your son to the wall."

"I'm afraid the good judge sealed her fate the moment he brought you into this."

"Then he'll come after you."

"You mean, after he gets over his grief? No doubt he'll try, but he'll have a hard time proving anything. As for vengeance of the more physical sort, I don't think he has it in him. You, on the other hand . . ." He shrugged. "But then, you're not in much of a position to do anything either. Are you?"

"Don't be so sure."

"Such bravado, Marshal. For someone who's given us such a chase, I'd have thought you could come up with something better than that. In fact, I really hadn't expected you to just come walking in here. You've made things so much easier for me and my men.

"Now, I have a particularly quiet, dark corner to store the two of you until we can dispose of you properly."

Kyle's jaw tightened.

Casale laughed again and moved to Jenny's side. "Did Munroe ever tell you about his particular aversion to dark, tight spaces?"

Jenny stared at the crime lord, unflinching.

"What about how he acquired that particular weakness?"

Before she could stop herself, she glanced at Kyle. One thing Kyle never talked about was his claustrophobia.

"I can see that he hasn't." Casale walked back to stand in front of Kyle. "Tsk, tsk, Marshal, keeping secrets from your lady love."

"Go to hell, Casale."

"Such wit. Certainly you can do better than that."

Returning to Jenny's side, Casale took her arm and led her to a chair next to Kyle. "You see, Miss Brooks, when Munroe here was very young, he had a particularly unpleasant experience. A group of gunmen took over a bank in Miami, and, unfortunately, Kathleen Munroe and her ten-year-old son happened to be in the bank that day. A case of being in the wrong place at the wrong time."

Casale crossed his arms and leaned back against his desk. "Along with twenty-five others, they were held hostage for six days. They were locked in an underground vault and given just enough food and water to live. But no light."

Casale paused, for effect no doubt. He watched Kyle, though his words were still addressed to Jenny.

"Actually, it was a brilliant strategy. You can imagine the demoralizing effects of being locked in a small space with twenty-four other people. They gave their captors no trouble.

"Unfortunately, three of the hostages died. Including Kathleen Munroe."

Jenny gasped, unable to stop herself. What a horrible thing for a ten-year-old child to live through.

"Yes, I agree," Casale said in mock sympathy. "Such a tragedy to see your mother die like that. Kyle, however, was made of sterner stuff. He lived. He's just never been too fond of small, tight spaces. But then"—Casale gave an elaborate shrug—"who can blame him?"

Jenny's heart ached for Kyle. Now she understood why he'd never spoken about his family or his youth. It would have been like reliving the horror of his mother's death every time.

"Well, I think that's about it," Casale said. "So, why don't you men take Miss Brooks and the marshal down to our special holding cell. And make sure Munroe doesn't cause any trouble."

Jenny watched in horror as one of the men brought down the butt of his gun on Kyle's head, knocking him unconscious.

This time the man kept a firm grip on Jenny's arm as he pulled her along behind the two men dragging Kyle. Again, they wound their way through endless hallways, then down several flights of stairs until the air itself told her they were underground in a part of the mansion that was decades older than the main house.

They finally stopped in front of a rough-hewn wooden door.

The man in the lead opened it, and the two holding Kyle tossed him in. He landed with a thud.

They shoved Jenny in after him, and she rushed to his side. She looked up at the men in the doorway, just as one of them lifted his gun and took aim at the single lightbulb in the center of the room. Jenny bent over Kyle, protecting his face from the shattering glass. Then the doors closed, the sounds of the laughter fading as they left Kyle and Jenny alone.

In the dark.

THIRTEEN

Kyle surfaced slowly, the pounding in his head a steady rhythm of agony.

"Can you hear me, Kyle?" It was an angel's voice, soft and pleading, pulling him upward. "Wake up."

He held on to the voice, moving toward it through a fog of pain.

"Please, Kyle." There were tears now, he could hear them, and a great sadness. "I need you."

He tried to get to her; had tried to hold on to her all his life. He'd wanted to protect her, to love her. He'd failed at both. And here she was again, pulling at him, pleading with him. This time he couldn't fail her.

He reached toward her, and awareness of his surroundings came slowly: a hard, cold floor, the sharp ache in his head, and long feminine fingers stroking his face.

Jenny.

He opened his eyes. And saw only darkness.

"Jenny?"

"Thank God, Kyle, you're awake." The tears fell on his face, and she pressed her lips against his briefly. "I was so worried. I thought you were dead. And then they hit you again."

"I can't see."

He sensed the walls. Close. Too close. And the panic slammed into him, hard and fast, threatening to send him back into the safety of unconsciousness. He fought it. He had to pull himself together for Jenny.

"They've locked us in some kind of cellar beneath the mansion," she said. "But, I'm here for you. Hold on to me."

Grabbing her hand, he anchored himself, adding her strength to his and bringing his fear under control. "I'm okay," he said a few moments later. "Tell me what happened."

"Not much after they knocked you out. They brought us down here. There was a light, but one of the men broke the bulb."

Kyle closed his eyes and could see Casale's smile. He planned to eliminate Kyle and Jenny. Yet, he'd put them here first, in a small, dark room, knowing what it would mean to Kyle.

"But how did he know?" Kyle hadn't meant to voice the question aloud.

"How did he know what?"

"About the bank and my mother." He opened

his eyes and tried to see Jenny's face in the darkness. "It's not in my personnel file in the department."

"Does it matter?"

"I'm not sure." He started to sit up.

Jenny shifted out from under him, and the terror crept in closer. Before it could take hold, she had an arm around his shoulders, helping him, chasing the fear away. Then the pain in his head washed over him again, and he went still for a moment, letting it settle.

"Are you okay?" she asked.

"Yeah." He took her hand again and squeezed it. "I'm not going to lose it on you, Jenny," he said, reinforcing his resolve with words. "I'm just a little shaky."

If only he could see her, even as a blurred outline or silhouette, it would help him master the panic. But the darkness was too complete. Instead, he reached out and touched her cheek, wincing at the dampness. "Are you okay? Did they hurt you?"

She turned her face into his hand and kissed his palm. "No, they didn't hurt me."

"We're not on our own, Jen. DeMitri knows we're here, and he'll come for us."

He could feel her faint smile against his hand and couldn't resist leaning over for one brief taste of those lips. She trembled as his mouth touched hers, and he drew back.

"Hey, what's with the tears?" He brought his other hand up to frame her face. "I'm the one who's supposed to fall apart." Brushing at the moisture with the flat of his thumbs, he said, "We're going to be okay. I promise."

"It's not that. I thought they'd killed you back in the parking lot."

"So did Casale." Kyle, of all people, knew how hard that must have been for her. Still, he tried to make light of it. "And Vittorio Casale doesn't like being wrong. I was wearing a vest. Government issue." He grinned. There would be time later for regrets and tears. *If* they survived. "Still hurt like a bitch, though."

Jenny laughed, and he kissed her. Longer this time, taking a moment to relish the sweet taste of her. Then he pulled back. "Come on, now. We need to try and get out of here."

"Sounds like a good idea to me. Any suggestions?"

"Let me get a feel for this room. Its size, contents, doors, windows. That sort of thing."

"I got a good look at it before they shot the light out. It's empty. Four concrete walls and one door."

"What about a window?" Although he knew it was too much to hope for. "Maybe painted over?"

"I don't think so . . ." She hesitated. "But I'm not sure."

"Okay, we're going to check."

He started to stand, and she slipped an arm around his waist, helping him. Again the pain made him unsteady for a moment, but it was easier to deal with than the thought of the four walls surrounding them.

"Kyle?"

He gave her shoulder a squeeze. "I'm okay. Let's get started."

They made their way across to the door, and Kyle checked it out from top to bottom, testing the lock and tracing the edges with his fingers.

"What are you looking for?" Jenny asked.

"If the hinges were on the inside, I thought I might be able to take the door down. But no such luck."

He started to move sideways, running his hands along the wall. "I'm going to work my way around the room. Jenny, stay with me and keep talking."

It didn't take him long to circle the area. It was small. Closet size. But he pushed that thought aside, visualizing instead a wide open expanse with plenty of space to breathe.

Jenny kept close the entire time, chatting about everything and nothing, keeping his fear of dark, closed spaces at bay with the sound of her voice and the feel of her nearby. She became his lifeline.

When he'd finished, they sat shoulder to shoulder on the floor against the far wall.

"Well, you're right," Kyle said, trying to keep the frustration out of his voice. "It's a solid, empty, concrete cell."

"There's no way out, is there?"

"Only through that doorway." Kyle reached over in the dark and found her hand. "Which means we need to be ready the next time it opens."

"Any ideas when that'll be?" He heard the fear in her voice and her struggle to control it.

He tried to give her hope. "Well, I figure it's about time for DeMitri to be knocking on the mansion doors."

"With a search warrant?"

"He was trying to get one when I left, but it didn't look good. There's no probable cause to link your kidnapping to Casale."

"But everyone knows he's behind this."

"That's not enough. Especially when dealing with a man as powerful as Casale. He's got everyone running scared."

"What about my father?"

"He's our best hope. But with or without a warrant, DeMitri will find an excuse to get to us." Kyle squeezed her hand. "I'd bet my life on it."

"I hate to mention this," she said, "but you *are* betting your life on it."

Kyle laughed abruptly and shifted to wrap his arm around her shoulders. Her courage continued to amaze him. "I guess I am at that. But, whether DeMitri comes through or not, Casale will send a couple of his hired guns down to take care of us. All we have to do is be ready when they get here."

"Well, at least we'll have the advantage of surprise."

Kyle smiled again at her optimism. "There is that."

"No really. You're forgetting something."

"Like?"

Jenny bent forward and pulled up one of the legs of her jeans. Before she'd finished, Kyle realized what she was going after.

"You still have the Colt? They didn't search you?"

Jenny withdrew the gun Samson had insisted she take with her when they'd left his cabin. "I guess it never occurred to them."

"You're incredible." Kyle pulled her into his arms. "Now we have a fighting chance."

After a while, the silence settled around them.

Kyle had come up with a plan that Jenny hoped would work. It sounded reasonable. All they needed was a break or two.

Meanwhile, they waited.

"Talk to me, Jenny," Kyle said.

"About what?" She knew the walls must be closing in on him.

"I don't care. Anything. It's too quiet in here."

She hesitated a moment, then said, "Can you tell me about your mother, Kyle?"

For several minutes he didn't answer, and she thought he'd refuse. Then he said, "As little as a week ago, I would have said no." He reached over and folded her hand between both of his. "Now . . . Maybe it's time."

She pulled their joined hands to her lips and kissed his fingers. "Only if you want to."

It took him a while to speak, as if he didn't know

how or where to start. "Sometimes at night," he said finally, "I wake up in the dark thinking I'm still there. The memory never lasts long, but in those few seconds I can still smell the dank, stale odors and hear the others. Some crying softly, while others, like my mother, prayed."

Jenny closed her eyes, aching for him; for the little boy he'd been and the man he'd become, both living with those memories.

He shifted, dropping her hands and wrapping an arm around her shoulder to pull her close.

"In Miami, August is a miserable month. Hot and humid. Mom had promised to take me to the beach that day, but she had to stop at the bank first." His fingers tightened against Jenny's upper arm. "We walked into the middle of a robbery gone wrong.

"We didn't know it at the time, but one of the tellers had tripped a silent alarm. Within minutes the police had surrounded the building, trapping the holdup men inside. But it backfired. Instead of surrendering, they took everyone in the bank hostage."

He shifted again, sitting straighter and stretching out his legs. "The rest is pretty much as Casale said. They locked us in the vault without light or air-conditioning, while they negotiated with the police for their freedom."

"It must have been terrible."

"Yeah. But it wasn't the deprivation or threats

that wore us down, it was the darkness and the heat."

"What happened to your mother?"

"Actually, it was an accident." She could hear his attempt to make light of it, as if the memory no longer bothered him. She knew better. She knew Kyle. He'd kept this buried inside so long because it was too painful to let out.

"One of the other hostages panicked. He wasn't much more than a boy himself. Or at least, I'm sure that's how my mother saw him. He was maybe twenty."

Kyle pulled his arm back, and Jenny felt its absence like a sudden chill. But she let it go, knowing he had to tell her this in his own way.

"Anyway," he continued, "about the fourth day, a group of us were being taken to the rest rooms when this kid freaked out. He started to run. The guard yelled for him to stop. I don't think he wanted to shoot anyone. Not really. But it was crazy. The boy screaming and yelling. The rest of us crying and calling for him to come back. The gunman taking aim and yelling at the same time. Then my mother stepped in front of the bullet."

"Oh, Kyle." Her voice caught in her throat, but he hurried on.

"She probably thought he wouldn't shoot a woman—if she thought about it at all."

For several minutes, neither of them spoke, while the anguish Kyle had revealed circled around them. Jenny could only guess how it had been for him. A few hours ago she'd watched him fall under a shotgun blast, and it had about destroyed her. How much worse for a child to see his mother gunned down.

Finally he turned to her and said, "So, there you have it. The whole story of my misspent youth." He took her hand and kissed it quickly. "Except for the part about how for the next few years I went a little bit wild. If there was trouble, I found it. That's when I met . . . Wait a minute. That's it!"

"What?" Jenny felt like she'd missed something important.

"That's how Casale knew about Samson. How he knew about both the bank *and* Samson."

"You knew Samson when you were a boy?"

"That wasn't his name, but yeah, he was a small-time crook, running a chop shop out of South Miami. When I was fifteen, I stole a car and tried to sell it to him. He turned me in, and I did six months in juvenile detention. As they say, it scared me straight.

"Those records were sealed. But hey, if Philip could hack into the Justice Department mainframe, Miami juvenile files must have been a cinch." She could sense his agitation, his excitement as he worked his way through the puzzle. "Philip must have cross-referenced the information in my juvenile file with the witness protection program's case files, looking for something he could use on me. Some way to get to you through me."

"Could he do that? Cross-reference the files like that?"

"It would be a simple enough program for a computer whiz like Philip. That's how he found out about Samson, whose real name is in my juvenile files. But the witness program's case files contain both the witness's real name and his assumed name. For Casale, it was a personal connection to one of my witnesses no one would have made otherwise."

"So—"

The sound of voices cut her off.

Jenny froze, fear pooling in the pit of her stomach. She felt Kyle tense and knew he'd heard them too. This was it. Casale's men were moving down the stairs, and they'd come to kill her and Kyle.

"It sounds like there's only two of them," he said, squeezing her hand. "That's good."

He pulled away from her, and she heard him pull the gun from his waistband and check the clip. Only a couple of days ago the weapon had appeared deadly to her. Now, it seemed small and totally inadequate for the job.

"Kyle . . ." she started.

"It's okay." He touched her cheek briefly. "You know what to do, right?"

Taking a deep breath, she nodded and said yes. She could do this. She could control her fear.

"Okay, then." He slipped a hand to the nape of her neck and pulled her to him for one quick kiss. When he released her, he said, "For luck."

For courage, she told herself. Aloud she said, "For luck."

One final squeeze of her hand, and he was gone. She tried to visualize him moving toward the side wall, lying down and curling up on his side like they'd planned.

He began to moan.

Jenny stood and braced herself against the back wall. She held on to the memory of his touch and the taste of his lips, hoping it would get her through the next few minutes.

Keys rattled in the lock, the door squeaked open, and a wash of light split the darkness of the room. Two of Casale's thugs stood on the threshold, though Jenny's eyes were too unaccustomed to the light to tell if she'd seen them before.

"Please," she said, finding it incredibly easy to sound desperate. "You need to get Kyle out of here. He can't deal with being locked in this small room. He's terrified."

One of the men laughed. "Oh, the marshal's afraid of the dark, is he? Too bad." She'd heard that voice before but couldn't place it. He stepped into the room, and she instinctively backed up—but there was nowhere to go.

"Well, it's going to be all over soon," he said. "And he won't have to be afraid anymore."

Jenny inched sideways, toward the far corner, putting as much distance as possible between herself and the doorway.

The man approached Kyle and nudged him

with his foot. "Come on, you, get up. We're going to take a little walk."

Kyle moaned louder, mumbling incoherently about darkness and walls closing in. He was so convincing, that for a moment, Jenny wondered if he'd actually succumbed to the terror.

Casale's man kicked Kyle again. Still he made no move to get up. "Come on, Marshal," he said. "Time's up." He leaned over and grabbed Kyle's arm.

It was a mistake.

In a flash, Kyle rolled over and rammed one booted foot into the man's knees, while taking aim and firing at the man still standing in the doorway. He missed the shot, but the first man went down, growling in pain. Kyle rammed an elbow into his chin, sending him sprawling and his flashlight and gun flying.

Jenny went for the gun, while Kyle dove for the man at the door, just as he raised his own gun and fired. The bullet went wild, and Kyle shoved the man backward, ramming his gun hand against the wall.

The first man struggled to stand, but Jenny shoved his own gun into his face. That's when she realized he was the shooter, the man who'd shot Kyle from the van.

Stepping back out of his reach, she lowered her aim. "Don't make the mistake of thinking I won't pull this trigger."

Something must have convinced him she meant it, because he sank back to the floor.

Kyle wrestled the gun from the man in the doorway and backed him into the room. That's when he saw that Jenny had taken up a shooter's stance over the man on the floor, the .357 Magnum in her hand aimed at the man's crotch.

Kyle inwardly winced. This guy had crossed the wrong woman.

"Here, let me have that now," he said, coming up alongside her and easing the gun from her hand.

The man actually looked relieved to be facing Kyle instead of Jenny, and Kyle almost laughed.

"Okay," he said, instead. "Let's get the keys and flashlight and get out of here."

A moment later they'd locked the two men in the room and started toward the stairs. At the top, Kyle motioned for Jenny to stay back. Using the tip of his gun, he pushed the door open carefully.

The hallway looked deserted.

Kyle guessed that DeMitri had arrived, throwing the household into turmoil. The two men downstairs had probably been sent to take Kyle and Jenny to some deserted place and kill them, while Casale made his escape.

Looking back at her, Kyle motioned toward the hallway. "It's clear for the moment. Let's go."

They worked their way down a long, empty corridor that seemed to run along the entire length of the house. Several doors led off toward their left, but none seemed to be a way out. Still, the longer they went without being challenged, the more sure Kyle became that Casale and his henchmen had fled.

Then he spotted the door to the pantry. Inside was the entrance to the stairway leading down to the root cellar where Casale's men had first cornered him. He was considering taking Jenny out that way when he heard voices coming from the direction of the front of the house.

DeMitri.

Grabbing Jenny's hand, he led her toward the sounds, but hung back at the entrance to the foyer until he was sure it was clear. He wasn't ready to take anything for granted anymore. Especially Jenny's safety.

DeMitri stood in the middle of the room, flanked by more than a dozen men—some in uniforms, others in suits. It seemed a lot of law enforcement types were eager for a chance to bring down Vittorio Casale.

"I have a warrant here to search the premises," DeMitri siad to a man Kyle hadn't seen before.

The stranger took the document from DeMitri and examined it. "It looks in order. I don't suppose there's any way I can stop you."

"No, there isn't." DeMitri nodded, and a half dozen men headed in as many directions. "I want to speak to Vittorio Casale."

"I'm afraid you've made a mistake, sir," said the man Kyle decided must be the butler—someone Casale kept separate from his minions with a more illegal bent. "This residence belongs to J. M. Smith. Not Mr. Casale."

"And where is this Mr. Smith?" DeMitri asked.

"I'm afraid he's out of the country at the moment."

DeMitri wasn't impressed. "And you have no knowledge of, nor have you seen Mr. Vittorio Casale?"

"Well, no." The butler suddenly seemed very uncomfortable. "I didn't say that. Mr. Casale often—"

Kyle had seen enough and stepped into the open. "Casale was just here."

DeMitri broke into a huge grin when he spotted them. "Munroe, glad to see you and Miss Brooks in one piece. You said Casale's been here?"

"My guess is he's making his escape as we speak."

"Spread out and find him," DeMitri ordered the remaining men at his side. Then turning back to the butler, he said, "I don't suppose you have any idea where I can find Mr. Casale."

"I couldn't say, sir."

"I'm sure you couldn't."

"I have a feeling I know where he's headed," Kyle said, suddenly remembering the unalarmed root cellar door. Propelling Jenny toward DeMitri, he said, "Watch her."

"Kyle . . ."

"Munroe . . ."

"And send some men around to the far west side

of the property," Kyle said over his shoulder, as he took off toward the back of the house.

It made sense. One door that wasn't wired into the central alarm system. It allowed entrance and *exit* of the house without anyone inside being the wiser. *If* you knew to watch for the laser sensor. Plus, the entrance to the root cellar was at the far end of the property, enough away from the main house to get some kind of vehicle in and out without being noticed.

Then Kyle reached the stairs leading down into the cellar and slowed, waiting for the first edges of panic to strike. Nothing. In a flash of relief so strong it staggered him, he realized that small, dark spaces no longer held any terror for him.

Jenny had done that. She'd chased away his demons.

Still, he proceeded carefully, knowing Casale would have left someone behind to cover his escape. Sure enough, as Kyle rounded on the landing, a bullet whizzed by his head. Flattening himself against the wall above the landing, he counted to three, swung out and fired. The man collapsed.

Kyle made it down the stairs in a few quick strides and grabbed the man's weapon. He'd been hit in the leg and shoulder, but he'd live.

Pocketing the extra automatic, Kyle hurried on, stopping again at the bottom of the outside staircase. The door had been carefully closed and locked, as if that would fool anyone into thinking Casale had taken another route.

Then Kyle heard the helicopter and knew his time had run out. Hurrying up the stairs, he came up behind Maxwell, the hired gun who'd grabbed Jenny. The other man spun around, and they faced off, each holding a weapon on the other.

"Ah, Munroe," Maxwell said, "still working alone I see."

"Give it up, this time the place *is* swarming with cops. You and your boss are going down."

"This time I believe you. About the police, anyway. As for the other, you need to get through me first."

"You want to die for a scumbag like Casale, that's your business." Kyle nodded toward two uniformed policemen who'd come up behind Maxwell, guns ready. "But I thought you were smarter than that."

Maxwell grinned. "I'm too smart to fall for that old trick."

One of the officers cocked his gun and said, "I hope so."

Maxwell's smile faded, but for a moment, he held his ground. Then he said, "Maybe you're right. I never was too fond of Vittorio." Lowering his gun, he nodded toward the far end of the building. "They're around the corner. The chopper should be just about ready to land."

"One of you watch him," Kyle said, "the other come with me."

He took off toward the sound of the approaching helicopter, coming out into the open just as it was about to touch down. Casale and three of his men stood off to the side.

"Cover me," he said to the man who'd followed him. Dropping to the ground, Kyle took aim and fired at the chopper's tail rotors. The four men spun around, guns in hand, but the officer at Kyle's side kept them busy. Kyle fired once. Twice. While clumps of dirt jumped up at him as bullets struck too close for comfort. But his third shot found its mark, and the helicopter dropped the last couple of feet to the earth. Kyle and the officer pulled back, ducking behind the building.

"Give it up, Casale! The place is swarming with cops."

Kyle mentally thanked DeMitri as a dozen men in uniform appeared from several different directions, taking up offensive positions around the four men and the crippled helicopter.

It was over in minutes.

Casale's three men evidently weren't willing to die for their boss. They threw down their guns and raised their hands.

Kyle closed the distance between them, with a half dozen uniforms on his heel. "You're under arrest, Casale," he said, as one of the policemen yanked the criminal's hands behind his back. "For kidnapping and attempted murder."

Casale remained impassive. Only his eyes showed his anger and his hate. "It'll never go to trial."

"I wouldn't count on that."

"Who's going to testify? You?"

"Why not?"

Casale arched an eyebrow and smiled. "Or maybe the judge's daughter?"

Kyle reined in the urge to kill Casale where he stood and save them all a lot of trouble. "Read him his rights," he said instead, and turned, heading back to the house.

To Jenny.

EPILOGUE

One of DeMitri's men drove Jenny and Kyle into Washington.

Someone had called ahead and told her father that she was safe, so there was no hurry. But she didn't want to wait. It had been too long, and the last few days had taught her the value of being near the ones she loved. She missed her father and didn't want to waste any more time before seeing him.

In the backseat of the car, she and Kyle sat close, his arm wrapped protectively around her shoulders. Neither of them spoke as they rode the last fifty miles of a journey that had taken them from Georgia to the shores of the Mississippi and then back to Washington, D.C. And in some ways, they'd gone so much farther.

She didn't know what was going to happen between them. What Kyle wanted to happen. Oh, she knew he desired her. In fact, she knew he loved her.

But how much? Enough to face all the demons they'd created together in the past and banish them? Enough for a lifetime?

All she knew for sure was what *she* wanted.

Kyle.

On whatever terms he'd have her.

Five years ago, she'd been a fool. She'd wanted a husband and been given a hero. He was a brave, good man, trying to make a difference in a crazy world. It would tear her apart if she lost him because of that. But it would be so much worse if she never had any time with him at all, if she turned her back on him because of her fear. She loved him, and whatever time they had, she'd relish.

As they pulled up in front of the courthouse and climbed out of the car, Jenny started laughing. "Kyle, look at us."

He checked her out from head to toe and then glanced at himself. "I guess we're not exactly dressed for court." He brushed at her cheek, and Jenny could imagine a smudge or two of dirt there. "In fact, we're not even very clean," he added.

Jenny felt like giggling. "You think my father will have a heart attack when he sees me like this?"

"You mean in those skintight jeans? Or maybe the leather jacket will set him off."

"Actually, I thought the boots would do it."

"You don't still have the Colt on you?"

Again, laughter bubbled inside her. "No, I gave it to DeMitri."

"Good. At least we'll make it through the metal detectors."

"Well then," she said, slipping her arm through his, "let's go make the judge throw us out."

They *did* get some odd stares as they entered the courthouse, a few pointed whispers and an occasional sniff, but no one stopped them. But then, Jenny thought, who would have the nerve to stop Kyle? He was a man on a mission—to deliver her to her father—and he looked it.

He took her to her father's courtroom and opened the door quietly. Still, several people turned as they entered, and a buzz spread through the room.

Philip Casale, sitting next to his high-priced attorney at the defendant's table, swiveled around, obviously puzzled at the interruption. He looked straight at her and Kyle, and she knew the moment he figured out who she was. His expression turned thunderous.

On the other hand, her father's gaze landed on Kyle with a frown but slid past her. Then he came back to her with a start, the surprise on his face almost comical. That's when Jenny remembered her hair, no longer honey-blond, but dark brown.

Kyle waited outside Crawford Brooks's chambers.

It hadn't taken the judge long to adjourn court for the day once he'd spotted his daughter in the back of the room. Then Kyle had escorted her to his chambers, delivering her into her father's arms. Kyle had backed off, letting the two of them have some time alone together.

Now he sat outside waiting, oblivious to the hard wooden bench and the long stretch of cold, empty hallway. He thought only of Jenny.

When he'd almost lost her, nothing else had mattered but getting her back alive. He hadn't done it because of his job, or so Crawford Brooks could give Philip Casale a fair trial. Hell, he hadn't even been doing it so Crawford Brooks would get his daughter back.

It had been personal.

It had been about Jenny. About saving a woman who'd been strong enough to stand up to one of the worst crime lords of their time. About saving the only woman he'd ever loved.

He couldn't—wouldn't—lose her again.

No matter what it took. There were other jobs, other less dangerous ways to make a living and a difference. He'd find one. Because having Jennifer Brooks by his side meant more to him than life itself.

Suddenly Jenny and her father walked out arm and arm, and Kyle sprang to his feet.

"There you are," she said, leaving her father's side for Kyle's. "I was wondering where you'd snuck off to." Before he could say anything she reached up, kissed him and slipped her arm through his.

A little startled, Kyle glanced at her father.

Crawford Brooks didn't even seem to notice. Extending his hand to Kyle, he said, "I want to thank you for saving my daughter's life."

"You're welcome, sir." Kyle shook the other man's hand before releasing it. "What's going to happen to Philip Casale?"

"Well, now that the personal connection between his father and Jennifer's disappearance has been established, I'll remove myself from the case. Another judge will be assigned."

Kyle nodded, knowing that would be for the best.

"I have a present for you," Jenny said, squeezing his arm. "Dad and I have been talking, and I've decided to testify against Vittorio Casale. The man's ego has finally gotten him into trouble. Instead of staying in the shadows as usual, he's made himself an easy target."

Kyle pulled back from her. "Jenny, you don't know what you're saying. Casale may be in custody, but this is far from over. He's still a very dangerous man."

"The only way it's ever going to be over," she said, "is if someone has the guts to stand up and testify against him." She squeezed his arm. "You taught me that."

He looked at her father for support. "Judge, you can't let her do this."

"It's no use," the older man said. "I've been

arguing with her for the past fifteen minutes. She's determined."

Turning back to Jenny, Kyle said, "There's no need for you to put yourself in more danger. I'll testify against Casale."

"You're a federal marshal who was caught breaking into his home," she said. "What kind of witness are you going to make? A good defense attorney will tear your testimony apart."

Kyle glanced at the judge and then back at her. "I don't want you to do this."

"I *want* to do it, Kyle."

"Look, no wife of mine is going to take the stand against Vittorio Casale. You've been through enough already."

Jenny laughed.

"What's so funny?" He glanced from Jenny to her father.

"I told you he loved me, Dad."

"I never doubted you."

"What's going on?" Kyle said.

Jenny threw her arms around him. "Wasn't that just a marriage proposal I heard?"

"It sounded like one to me," Crawford said.

"Jenny, you're changing the subject."

"You don't want to marry me?"

"Of course, I want to marry you. I'm going to resign from the marshal service. We can go back to Atlanta or wherever you want."

"There's no need to go back to Atlanta. I can get a job here just as easily. And you're definitely *not* going to resign." She kissed him on the cheek. "Unless you want someone else to take me into protective custody when I testify."

"Jenny . . ." He put a warning in his voice, but she didn't seem inclined to hear it. "We were talking about Casale."

"We were talking about getting married." She smiled suggestively. "Preferably before Casale goes to trial."

Frustrated, Kyle looked down into her honey-brown eyes and realized he wasn't going to change her mind. She was going to testify against Vittorio Casale, whether Kyle approved or not. And he couldn't help but love her more for it.

"So," he said, glancing from her to her father and back again, "do you know of anyone willing to perform this marriage ceremony for us?"

She smiled up at him, and he thought he'd never seen a lovelier sight. "Oh, I think I know a judge who might agree."

He answered her smile with one of his own and brushed his lips against hers. "Good. Because I don't want to wait."

"I love you, too, Kyle."

THE EDITORS' CORNER

Men. We love 'em, we hate 'em, but when it comes right down to it, we can't get along without 'em. Especially the ones we may never meet: those handsome guys with the come-hither eyes, those gentle giants with the hearts of gold, those debonair men who make you want to say yes. Well, this October you'll get your chance to meet those very men. Their stories make up LOVESWEPT's MEN OF LEGEND month. There's nothing like reuniting with an old flame, and the men our four authors have picked will definitely have you shivering with delight!

Marcia Evanick presents the final chapter in her White Lace & Promises trilogy, **HERE'S LOOKIN' AT YOU**, LOVESWEPT #854. Morgan De Witt promised his father that he would take care of his sister, Georgia. Now that Georgia's happily engaged, he's facing a lonely future and has decided it's time to find a Mrs. De Witt. Enter Maddie Andrews. Years ago, Maddie offered Morgan her heart, and he rebuffed the gawky fifteen-year-old. Morgan can't understand why Maddie is so aloof, but he's determined to crack her defenses, even if he has to send her the real Maltese Falcon to do so. Maddie's heart melts every time he throws in a line or two from her favorite actor, but can she overcome the fears bedeviling her every thought of happiness? As usual, Marcia Evanick delights readers with a love that is at times difficult, but always, always enduring.

Loveswept favorite Sandra Chastain returns with **MAC'S ANGELS: SCARLET LADY**, LOVE-SWEPT #855. Rhett Butler Montana runs his riverboat casino like the rogue he was named for, but when a mysterious woman in red breaks the bank and then dares him to play her for everything he owns, he's sorely tempted to abandon his Southern gentility in favor of a little one-on-one. With her brother missing and her family's plantation at stake, Katie Carithers has her own agenda in mind; she must form an uneasy alliance with the gambler who's bound by honor to help any damsel in distress. As the two battle over integrity, family, and loyalty, Katie and Rhett discover that what matters most is not material but intangible—that thing called love. Sandra Chastain ignites a fiery duel of wits and wishes when she sends a sexy rebel to do battle with his leading lady.

Next up is Stephanie Bancroft's delightful tale of Kat McKray and James Donovan, the former British agent who boasts a **LICENSE TO THRILL**, LOVESWEPT #856. Even though James Donovan is known the world over as untouchable and hard to hold, he has never lacked for companionship of the female persuasion. But after delivering a letter of historic consequence to the curvaceous museum curator, James is sure his sacred state of bachelorhood is doomed. Kat refuses to lose her heart to another love 'em and leave 'em kind of guy, a vow that slowly dissolves in the wake of James's presence. When Kat is arrested in the disappearance of the valuable artifact, it's up to James to save Kat's reputation and find the true culprit. In a romantic caper that taps into every woman's fantasy of 007 in hot pursuit, Stephanie keeps the pulse racing with a woman desperate to clear her name and that of the spy who loves her.

Talk about a tall tale! Donna Kauffman delivers **LIGHT MY FIRE,** LOVESWEPT #857, a novel about a smoke jumper and a maverick agent whose strength and determination are matched only by each other's. Larger than life, 6′ 7″ T. J. Delahaye rescues people for a living and enjoys it. By no means a shrinking violet at 6′ 2″, Jenna King rescues the environment and is haunted by it. But you know what they say—the bigger they are, the harder they fall—and these two are no exception. Trapped by the unrelenting forces of nature, Jenna and T. J. must rely on instinct and each other to survive. Sorrow has touched them both deeply, and if they make it through this ordeal alive, will they put aside the barriers long enough to learn the secret thrill of surrender? In a story fiercely erotic and deeply moving, Donna draws the reader into an inferno of emotion and fans the flames high with the heat of heartbreaking need.

Happy reading!

With warmest regards,

Susann Brailey   *Joy Abella*

Susann Brailey   Joy Abella

Senior Editor   Administrative Editor

P.S. Look for these Bantam women's fiction titles coming in October. From Jane Feather, Patricia Coughlin, Sharon & Tom Curtis, Elizabeth Elliott, Patricia Potter, and Suzanne Robinson comes **WHEN YOU WISH . . .** , a collection of truly romantic tales, in which a mysterious bottle containing one wish falls into the hands of each of the heroines . . . with magical results. Hailed by *Romantic Times* as "an exceptional talent with a tremendous gift for involving her readers in the story," Jane Ashford weaves a historical romance between Ariel Harding and the Honorable Alan Gresham, an unlikely alliance that will lead to the discovery of a dark truth and unexpected love in **THE BARGAIN**. National bestselling author Kay Hooper intertwines the lives of two women, strangers who are drawn together by one fatal moment, in **AFTER CAROLINE**. Critically acclaimed author Glenna McReynolds offers us **THE CHALICE AND THE BLADE**, the romantic fantasy of Ceridwen and Dain, struggling to escape the dangers and snares set by friend and foe alike, while discovering that neither can resist the love that promises to bind them forever. And immediately following this page, take a sneak peek at the Bantam women's fiction titles on sale in August.

DARK PARADISE
by **Tami Hoag**

Here is nationally bestselling author Tami Hoag's breathtakingly sensual novel, a story filled with heart-stopping suspense and shocking passion . . . a story of a woman drawn to a man as hard and untamable as the land he loves, and to a town steeped in secrets—where a killer lurks.

She could hear the dogs in the distance, baying relentlessly. Pursuing relentlessly, as death pursues life.

Death.

Christ, she was going to die. The thought made her incredulous. Somehow, she had never really believed this moment would come. The idea had always loitered in the back of her mind that she would somehow be able to cheat the grim reaper, that she would be able to deal her way out of the inevitable. She had always been a gambler. Somehow, she had always managed to beat the odds. Her heart fluttered and her throat clenched at the idea that she would not beat them this time.

The whole notion of her own mortality stunned her, and she wanted to stop and stare at herself, as if she were having an out-of-body experience, as if this person running were someone she knew only in passing. But she couldn't stop. The sounds of the dogs drove her on. The instinct of self-preservation spurred her to keep her feet moving.

She lunged up the steady grade of the mountain, tripping over exposed roots and fallen branches. Brush grabbed her clothing and clawed her bloodied face like gnarled, bony fingers. The carpet of decay on the forest floor gave way in spots as she scrambled, yanking her back precious inches instead of giving her purchase to propel herself forward. Pain seared through her as her elbow cracked against a stone half buried in the soft loam. She picked herself up, cradling the arm against her body, and ran on.

Sobs of frustration and fear caught in her throat and choked her. Tears blurred what sight she had in the moon-silvered night. Her nose was broken and throbbing, forcing her to breathe through her mouth alone, and she tried to swallow the cool night air in great gulps. Her lungs were burning, as if every breath brought in a rush of acid instead of oxygen. The fire spread down her arms and legs, limbs that felt like leaden clubs as she pushed them to perform far beyond their capabilities.

I should have quit smoking. A ludicrous thought. It wasn't cigarettes that was going to kill her. In an isolated corner of her mind, where a strange calm resided, she saw herself stopping and sitting down on a fallen log for a final smoke. It would have been like those nights after aerobics class, when the first thing she had done outside the gym was light up. Nothing like that first smoke after a workout. She laughed, on the verge of hysteria, then sobbed, stumbled on.

The dogs were getting closer. They could smell the blood that ran from the deep cut the knife had made across her face.

There was no one to run to, no one to rescue her. She knew that. Ahead of her, the terrain only turned more rugged, steeper, wilder. There were no people, no roads. There was no hope.

Her heart broke with the certainty of that. No hope. Without hope, there was nothing. All the other systems began shutting down.

She broke from the woods and stumbled into a clearing. She couldn't run another step. Her head swam and pounded. Her legs wobbled beneath her, sending her lurching drunkenly into the open meadow. The commands her brain sent shorted out en route, then stopped firing altogether as her will crumbled.

Strangling on despair, on the taste of her own blood, she sank to her knees in the deep, soft grass and stared up at the huge, brilliant disk of the moon, realizing for the first time in her life how insignificant she was. She would die in this wilderness, with the scent of wildflowers in the air, and the world would go on without a pause. She was nothing, just another victim of another hunt. No one would even miss her. The sense of stark loneliness that thought sent through her numbed her to the bone.

No one would miss her.

No one would mourn her.

Her life meant nothing.

She could hear the crashing in the woods behind her. The sound of hoofbeats. The snorting of a horse. The dogs baying. Her heart pounding, ready to explode.

She never heard the shot.

FROM THE *New York Times* BESTSELLING

BETINA KRAHN

With the wit of *The Last Bachelor*, the charm of *The Perfect Mistress*, and the sparkle of *The Unlikely Angel*, Betina Krahn has penned an enchanting new romance

THE MERMAID

If Celeste Ashton hadn't needed money to save her grandmother's seaside estate, she would never have published her observations on ocean life and the dolphins she has befriended. So when her book makes her an instant celebrity, she is unprepared for the attention . . . especially when it comes from unnervingly handsome Titus Thorne. While Titus suspects there is something fishy about her theories, Celeste is determined to be taken seriously. Soon their fiery ideological clashes create sparks neither expects, and Titus must decide if he will risk his credibility, his career—and his heart—to side with the Lady Mermaid.

"KRAHN HAS A DELIGHTFUL, SMART TOUCH."
—*Publishers Weekly*

"Miss Ashton, permit me to apologize for what may appear to one outside the scientific community to be rudeness on the part of our members. We are all accustomed to the way the vigorous spirit of inquiry often leads to enthusiastic questioning and debate. The familiarity of long acquaintance and the dogged pursuit of truth sometimes lead us to overstep the bounds of general decorum."

She stared at the tall, dark-haired order bringer, uncertain whether to be irritated or grateful that he had just taken over her lecture.

"I believe I . . . understand."

Glancing about the lecture hall, she was indeed beginning to understand. She had received their invitation to speak as an honor, and had prepared her lecture under the assumption that she was being extended a coveted offer of membership in the societies. But, in fact, she had not been summoned here to *join;* she had been summoned here to *account.* They had issued her an invitation to an inquisition . . . for the grave offense of publishing research without the blessing of the holy orders of science: the royal societies.

"Perhaps if I restated a few of the questions I have heard put forward just now," he said, glancing at the members seated around him, "it would preserve order and make for a more productive exchange."

Despite his handsome smile and extreme mannerliness, her instincts warned that here was no ally.

"You state that most of your observations have been made while you were in the water with the creatures, themselves." As he spoke, he made his way to the end of the row, where the others in the aisle made way for him to approach the front of the stage.

"That is true," she said, noting uneasily the way the others parted for him.

"If I recall correctly, you stated that you sail or row out into the bay waters, rap out a signal on the hull of your boat, and the dolphin comes to greet you. You then slip into the water with the creature—or creatures, if he has brought his family group—hold your breath, and dive under the water to observe them."

"That is precisely what happens. Though I must say, it is a routine perfected by extreme patience and long experience. Years, in fact."

"You expect us to believe you not only call these creatures at will, but that you voluntarily . . . single-handedly . . . climb into frigid water with any number of these monstrous large beasts, and that you swim underwater for hours on end to observe them?" He straightened, glancing at the others as he readied his thrust. "That is a great deal indeed to believe on the word of a young woman who has no scientific training and no formal academic background."

His words struck hard and sank deep. So that was it. She was young and female and intolerably presumptuous to attempt to share her learning and experiences with the world when she hadn't the proper credentials.

"It is true that I have had no formal academic training. But I studied and worked with my grandfather for years; learning the tenants of reason and logic, developing theoretical approaches, observing and recording." She stepped out from behind the podium, facing him, facing them all for the sake of what she knew to be the truth.

"There is much learning, sir, to be had *outside* the hallowed, ivy-covered walls of a university. Experience is a most excellent tutor."

She saw him stiffen as her words found a mark in him. But a moment later, all trace of that fleeting reaction was gone.

"Very well, Miss Ashton, let us proceed and see what your particular brand of science has produced." His words were now tightly clipped, tailored for maximum impact. "You observe underwater, do you not? Just how do you *see* all of these marvels several yards beneath the murky surface?"

"Firstly, ocean water is not 'murky.' Anyone who has spent time at the seaside knows that." She moved to the table and picked up a pair of goggles. "Secondly, I wear these. They are known in sundry forms to divers on various continents."

"Very well, it might work. But several obstacles still remain. Air, for instance. How could you possibly stay under the water long enough to have seen all that you report?"

She looked up at him through fiercely narrowed eyes.

"I hold my breath."

"Indeed? Just how long can you hold your breath, Miss Ashton?"

"Minutes at a time."

"Oh?" His eyebrows rose. "And what proof do you have?"

"Proof? What proof do you need?" she demanded, her hands curling into fists at her sides. "Shall I stick my head in a bucket for you?"

Laughter skittered through their audience, only to die when he shot them a censuring look. "Perhaps we could arrange an impromptu test of your remarkable breathing ability, Miss Ashton. I propose that you hold your breath—right here, right now—and we will time you."

"Don't be ridiculous," she said, feeling crowded by his height and intensity. He stood head and shoulders above her and obviously knew how to use his size to advantage in a confrontation.

"It is anything *but* ridiculous," he declared. "It would be a demonstration of the repeatability of a phenomenon. Repetition of results is one of the key tests of scientific truth, is it not?"

"It would not be a true trial," she insisted, but loathe to mention why. His silence and smug look combined with derogatory comments from the audience to prod it from her. "I am wearing a 'dress improver,'" she said through clenched teeth, "which restricts my breathing."

"Oh. Well." He slid his gaze down to her waist, allowing it to linger there for a second too long. When she glared at him, he smiled. "We can adjust for that by giving you . . . say . . . ten seconds?"

Before she could protest, he called for a mirror to detect stray breath. None could be found on such short notice, so, undaunted, he volunteered to hold a strip of paper beneath her nose to detect any intake of air. The secretary, Sir Hillary, was drafted as a timekeeper and a moment later she was forced to purge her lungs, strain her corset to take in as much air as possible, and then hold it.

Her inquisitor leaned close, holding that fragile strip of paper, watching for the slightest flutter in it. And as she struggled to find the calm center into which she always retreated while diving, she began to feel the heat radiating from him . . . the warmth of his face near her own . . . the energy coming from his broad shoulders. And she saw his eyes, mere inches from hers, beginning to wander over her face. Was he purposefully trying to distract her? Her quickening pulse said that if he was, his tactic was working. To combat it, she searched desperately for someplace to fasten her vision, something to concentrate on. Unfortunately, the closest available thing was *him*.

Green eyes, she realized, with mild surprise. Blue

green, really. The color of sunlight streaming into the sea on a midsummer day. His skin was firm and lightly tanned . . . stretched taut over a broad forehead, high cheekbones, and a prominent, slightly aquiline nose. Her gaze drifted downward to his mouth . . . full, velvety looking, with a prominent dip in the center of his upper lip that made his mouth into an intriguing bow. There were crinkle lines at the corners of his eyes and a beard shadow was forming along the edge of his cheek.

She found herself licking her lip . . . lost in the bold angles and intriguing textures of his very male face . . . straining for control and oblivious to the fact that half of the audience was on its feet and moving toward the stage. She had never observed a man this close for this long—well, besides her grandfather and the brigadier. A man. A handsome man. His hair was a dark brown, not black, she thought desperately. And as her chest began to hurt, she fastened her gaze on his eyes and held on with everything in her. This was for science. This was for her dolphins. This was to teach those sea green eyes a lesson . . .

The ache in her chest gradually crowded everything but him and his eyes from her consciousness. Finally, when she felt the dimming at the edges of her vision, which spelled real danger, she blew out that breath and then gasped wildly. The fresh air was so intoxicating that she staggered.

A wave of astonishment greeted the news that she had held her breath for a full three minutes.

BRIDE OF DANGER
by **Katherine O'Neal**

Winner of the *Romantic Times* Award for Best
Sensual Historical Romance

*Night after night, she graced London's most elegant
soirees, her flame-haired beauty drawing all eyes, her
innocent charm wresting from men the secrets of their
souls. And not one suspected the truth: that she was a
spy, plucked from the squalor of Dublin's filthy streets.
For Mylene, devoted to the cause of freedom, it was a
role she gladly played . . . until the evening she came
face-to-face with the mysterious Lord Whitney. All of the
ton was abuzz with his recent arrival. But only Mylene
knew he was as much of an imposter as she. Gone was
any trace of Johnny, the wild Irish youth she
remembered. In his place was a rogue more devastatingly
handsome than any man had a right to be—and a rebel
coldheartedly determined to do whatever it took to fulfill
his mission. Now he was asking Mylene to betray
everything she'd come to believe in. And even as she
knew she had to stop him, she couldn't resist
surrendering to his searing passion.*

On the boat to England, Mylene had learned her role.
She was to play an English orphan who'd lost her
parents in an Irish uprising and, for want of any rela-
tions, had been shipped home to an English orphan-
age. The story would explain Mylene's knowledge of
Dublin. But more, it was calculated to stir the embers
of her adoptive father Lord Stanley's heart. He was
the staunchest opposition Parliament had to Irish
Home Rule. That Mylene's parents had been killed

by Irish rabble rousers garnered his instant sympathy. He'd taken her in at first glance, and formally adopted her within the year.

In the beginning, Mylene had been flabbergasted by her surroundings. She wasn't certain she could perform such an extended role without giving herself away. The luxurious lifestyle, the formalities and graces, proved matters of extreme discomfort. To be awakened in the warmth of her plush canopied bed with a cup of steaming cocoa embarrassed her as much as being waited on hand and foot. But soon enough, James—the driver who secretly worked for their cause—had passed along her assignment. She was to use her position to discover the scandalous secrets of Lord Stanley's friends and associates. Buoyed by the sense of purpose, she'd thrown herself into her task with relish, becoming accomplished at the subterfuge in no time.

What she hadn't counted on was growing to love Lord Stanley. Ireland, and her old life, began to seem like the dream.

"How fares the Countess?" he asked, thinking she'd gone to visit a friend.

"Well enough, I think, for all that her confinement makes her edgy."

"Well, it's all to a good purpose, as she'll see when the baby comes. But tell me, my dear, did her happy state have its effect? I shouldn't mind a grandchild of my own before too much time."

"The very thing we were discussing when you came in," announced his companion.

Mylene turned and looked at Roger Helmsley. He was a dashing gentleman of thirty years, tall with dark brown hair and a fetching pencil-thin mustache. He wore his evening clothes with negligent ease, secure in his wealth and position. He was Lord Stanley's compatriot in Parliament, the driving force behind the Irish opposition.

"Lord Helmsley has been pressing his suit," explained her father. "He informs me, with the most dejected of countenances, that he's asked for your hand on three separate occasions. Yet he says you stall him with pretty smiles."

"She's a coy one, my lord," said Roger, coming to take both her hands in his. "I daresay some of your own impeccable diplomacy has rubbed off on your daughter."

"Is this a conspiracy?" she laughed. "Is a girl not to be allowed her say?"

"If you'd say anything at all, I might bear up. But this blasted silence on the subject . . . Come, my sweet. What must an old bachelor like myself do to entice the heart of such a fair maiden?"

Roger was looking at her with a glow of appreciation that to this day made her flush with wonder. At twenty-two, Mylene had blossomed under the Earl's care. The rich food from his table had transformed the scrawny street urchin into a woman with enticing curves. Her breasts were full, her hips ripe and rounded, her legs nicely lean and defined from hours in the saddle and long walks through Hyde Park. Her skin, once so sallow, glowed with rosy health. Even her riotous curls glistened with rich abundance. Her pouty mouth was legendary among the swells of Marlboro House. Her clothes were fashioned by the best dressmakers in London, giving her a regal, polished air—if one didn't look too closely at the impish scattering of freckles across her nose. But when she looked in the mirror, she always gave a start of surprise. She thought of herself still as the ill-nourished orphan without so much as a last name.

It was partly this quest for a family of her own that had her considering Roger's proposal. He was an affable and decent man who, on their outings, had displayed a free-wheeling sense of the absurd that had brought an element of fun to her sadly serious life. His wealth, good looks, and charm were the talk of mothers with marriageable daughters. And if his politics appalled her, she'd learned long ago from Lord Stanley that a man could hold differing, even dangerous political views, and still be the kindest of men. Admittedly, the challenge intrigued her. As his wife, she could perhaps influence him to take a more liberal stance.

"You see how she avoids me," Roger complained in a melodramatic tone.

There was a knock on the door before the panels were slid open by Jensen, the all-too-proper major-domo who'd been in the service of Lord Stanley's grandfather. "Excuse the intrusion, my lord, but a gentleman caller awaits your pleasure without."

"A caller?" asked Lord Stanley. "At this hour?"

"His card, my lord."

Lord Stanley took the card. "Good gracious. Lord Whitney. Send him in, Jensen, by all means."

When Jensen left with a stiff bow, Roger asked, "A jest perhaps? A visit from the grave?"

"No, no, my good man. Not old Lord Whitney. It's his son. I'd heard on his father's death that he was on his way. Been in India with his mother since he was a lad. As you know, the climate agreed with her, and she refused to return when her husband's service was at an end. Kept the boy with her. We haven't seen the scamp since he was but a babe."

"Well, well, this *is* news! It's our duty, then, to set

him straight right from the start. Curry his favor, so to speak. We shouldn't want the influence he's inherited to go the wrong way."

"He's his father's son. He'll see our way of things, I'll warrant."

Mylene knew what this meant. Old Lord Whitney, while ill and with one foot in the grave, had nevertheless roused himself to Parliament in his wheelchair to lambaste, in his raspy voice, the MPs who favored Ireland's pleas. Lord Stanley, she knew, was counting on the son to take up the cause. It meant another evening of feeling her hackles rise as the gentlemen discussed new ways to squelch the Irish rebellion.

She kept her lashes lowered, cautioning herself to silence, as the gentleman stepped into the room and the doors were closed behind him.

Lord Stanley greeted him. "Lord Whitney, what a pleasant surprise. I'd planned to call on you myself, as soon as I'd heard you'd arrived. May I express my condolences for your father's passing. He was a distinguished gentleman, and a true friend. I assure you, he shall be missed by all."

Mylene felt the gentleman give a gracious bow.

"Allow me to present my good friend, Lord Helmsley. You'll be seeing a great deal of each other, I don't doubt."

The men shook hands.

"And this, sir, is my daughter, Mylene. Lord Whitney, from India."

Mylene set her face in courteous lines. But when she glanced up, the smile of welcome froze on her face.

It was Johnny!

On sale in September:

AFTER CAROLINE
by Kay Hooper

WHEN YOU WISH . . .
by Jane Feather, Patricia Coughlin, Sharon & Tom Curtis, Elizabeth Elliot, Patricia Potter, and Suzanne Robinson

THE BARGAIN
by Jane Ashford

THE CHALICE AND THE BLADE
by Glenna McReynolds

DON'T MISS THESE FABULOUS
BANTAM WOMEN'S FICTION TITLES

On Sale in August

DARK PARADISE
by TAMI HOAG,
The New York Times *bestselling author of* GUILTY AS SIN

A breathtakingly sensual novel filled with heart-stopping suspense and shocking passion . . . a story of a woman drawn to a man as hard and untamable as the land he loves, and to a town steeped in secrets—where a killer lurks.   ____ 56161-8 $6.50/$8.99

THE MERMAID
by New York Times *bestseller* BETINA KRAHN,
author of THE UNLIKELY ANGEL

An enchanting new romance about a woman who works with dolphins in Victorian England and an academic who must decide if he will risk his career, credibility—and his heart—to side with the Lady Mermaid.
   ____ 57617-8 $5.99/$7.99

BRIDE OF DANGER
by KATHERINE O'NEAL,
winner of the Romantic Times *Award*
for Best Sensual Historical Romance

A spellbinding adventure about a beautiful spy who graces London's most elegant soirees and a devastatingly handsome rebel who asks her to betray everything she has come to believe in.   ____ 57379-9 $5.99/$7.99

DON'T MISS THESE FABULOUS BANTAM WOMEN'S FICTION TITLES

On Sale in September

AFTER CAROLINE by Kay Hooper

A sensuous novel about the bewildering connection between two strangers who look enough alike to be twins. When one of them mysteriously dies, the survivor searches for the truth—was Caroline's death an accident, or was she the target of a killer willing to kill again?

___57184-2 $5.99/$7.99

WHEN YOU WISH...
by Jane Feather, Patricia Coughlin, Sharon & Tom Curtis, Elizabeth Elliott, Patricia Potter, and Suzanne Robinson

National bestseller Jane Feather leads a talent-packed line-up in this enchanting collection of six original—and utterly romantic—short stories. A mysterious bottle containing one wish falls into the hands of each of the heroines...with magical results.

___57643-7 $5.99/$7.99

THE BARGAIN
by Jane Ashford, author of THE MARRIAGE WAGER

When a maddeningly forthright beauty and an arrogant, yet undeniably attractive scientist team up to rid London of a mysterious ghost, neither plans on the most confounding of all scientific occurrences: the breathless chemistry of desire.

___57578-3 $5.99/$7.99

THE CHALICE AND THE BLADE
by Glenna McReynolds

In a novel of dark magic, stirring drama, and fierce passion, the daughter of a Druid priestess and a feared sorcerer unlock the mystery of an ancient legacy.

___10384-9 $16.00/$22.95

- -

Ask for these books at your local bookstore or use this page to order.

Please send me the books I have checked above. I am enclosing $____ (add $2.50 to cover postage and handling). Send check or money order, no cash or C.O.D.'s, please.

Name _____

Address _____

City/State/Zip _____

Send order to: Bantam Books, Dept. FN158, 2451 S. Wolf Rd., Des Plaines, IL 60018

Allow four to six weeks for delivery.

Prices and availability subject to change without notice.   FN 158 9/97